Books by Alisa Allan

WINDS OF CHANGE - ISBN: 0-9761480-0-5
Cruise to Bermuda with a young woman who is forced to choose.
Rekindle a past?... Or set it free?

AFTER MIDNIGHT - ISBN: 0-9761480-1-3
Cruise to the Mexican Riviera and the Canada/New England coast with
two strangers who marry and clash in a blaze of differences.

THE BEST MAN - ISBN: 0-9761480-2-1
Cruise to Hawaiian Island paradise with a woman caught up in a
tailspin of revenge after a failed wedding attempt, and finds herself in
the middle of a bond that could not be broken.

BEYOND THE HORIZON - ISBN: 0-9761480-3-X
Cruise to the Caribbean with three friends who are taken away by
balmy tropical breezes and become vulnerable to its magic, then
discover a web of lies and deceit underneath its beauty.

ONE LAST TIME - ISBN: 0-9761480-4-8
Cruise to the Caribbean with a single mother and her son as they set off
on a journey of adventure. Immersed in exotic ambiance, a woman lets
go of a battle that threatens to drown her, but must eventually return
and face it, and she must risk all she found to face it alone.

ANGEL MIST - ISBN: 0-9761480-5-6
Cruise to Alaska as a young woman discovers a calm to the haunts of
her past, but she finds she would truly have to go home again before
she could find real peace.

Visit us:
www.BonVoyageBooks.com
www.TravelTimePress.com
www.AlisaAllan.com

ANGEL MIST

Alisa Allan

Bon Voyage Books
An Imprint of Travel Time Press

Bon Voyage Books
An Imprint of Travel Time Press

Angel Mist
Copyright © 2005 Alisa Allan, All Rights Reserved

ISBN: 0-9761480-5-6

Visit us
www.BonVoyageBooks.com
www.TravelTimePress.com
www.AlisaAllan.com

Publisher SAN# 2 5 6 – 5 7 9 X

ONE SHOULD COUNT EACH DAY, A SEPARATE LIFE

CHAPTER ONE

Morgan's mind was elsewhere, had been for several days, and a restless feeling plagued her as she tried to enjoy dinner with Evan.

"Something else on your mind?"

"What?" She looked up from her plate of food she hadn't touched.

"You haven't heard a word I've said."

Morgan smiled apologetically. "I'm sorry, say it again and I'll pay attention this time, I promise."

"I was talking about the upcoming conference."

"Oh, I'm not going. Are you?"

Evan laughed. "I said I was, that was the part you weren't paying attention to. I wasn't going to but Ray promised a great place for golf, and I could use the break," he poured her another glass of wine. "What are you thinking about tonight?"

She shrugged her shoulders. "Nothing in particular, it's been a long day. I had three births today and that of course puts my patients that were due in for office visits over to tomorrow, so I'm looking at pushing two days work into one."

"That's the kind of schedule you thrive on." He knew it wasn't about a double work load, she always took on anything that came her way and most times wanted more. "Maybe you should think about the conference."

"I don't have time. I'm a working doctor, Evan, with a busy practice in the city. You country doctor's have much more flexible spare time."

"It's a different pace, I'll give you that. But you could use the time away."

"What are you doing in the city anyway? I was surprised to get your message," she changed the subject, Morgan wasn't interested in going anywhere, she needed the work to get her mind back on track as lately it had a tendency to wander to things she didn't want to think about.

"Maybe I came to the city just to see you?"

"But you didn't."

Evan smiled. "I needed to consult with someone at the hospital, a patient is having a rougher time with some bone healing than he should be."

"I can't help you there. I bring the babies into the world and it's up to the rest of the medical community to fix them through life. Any prognosis?"

"Not yet," he answered, and then went back to their initial conversation she tried to change. "The conference is one of the best of the year, I'm hoping to gather more insight, there are a few class sessions that..."

"Have a wonderful time and send me a postcard," she interrupted him with a smile.

"When was the last time you had a little vacation time?"

She couldn't remember when, but didn't tell him that. "It hasn't been that long ago."

"Where did you go?" Evan tested.

"Somewhere."

"You drive yourself too hard, I'm only looking out for you and I think it would be good for you."

She sighed. "There are quite a few things that are good for me that I don't have time for."

"Eating right is one of them and you haven't touched a thing."

"Why are you worrying about me so?"

Evan looked at her and wasn't quite sure what to answer. Just an instinct he had, just a feeling that something wasn't right with her lately. "I think something is wrong and you're not telling me. You've been distracted lately, it isn't because you had a bad day, it isn't because you don't want to talk about the conference, and it isn't the dinner you've barely touched, what's on your mind?" He paused but she said nothing. "You're not going to tell me what it is, are you?"

She couldn't tell him what she was thinking about, she really wasn't sure. Her thoughts wandered to things she didn't want to think about, things she always stopped herself from thinking about, only lately that had been difficult. It was as if something in the back of her mind was literally pushing it to the forefront and forcing it upon her. And it didn't help that when she left Evan and returned home, there was a message from her mother.

"Morgan, this is Mom." She paused briefly, hoped that Morgan was there and would pick up the phone, then continued into the answering machine. "I guess you're not there. Well, it isn't important, I know you're busy."

She looked at her watch and knew it would be too late to call now, she was sure her mother had long since been in bed. It was a viable excuse anyway, she told herself. She'd call her tomorrow, or the next day, put it off as long as possible, her mother said it wasn't important so there was no urgency. After listening to the rest of the messages, one from her best friend Nancy and one from an associate who wanted her to take his patients while he was away, she turned the machine off and prepared herself for the long dark night ahead.

It had been so difficult to sleep lately, Morgan had to work to a point of near exhaustion before she could get a halfway restful night, she'd do paperwork, have a late work out at the gym down the street, even went so far as to volunteer to be on call when she didn't need to be. All of it in an effort to help her body shut down for rest, but lately nothing seemed to work, and she knew that night would be no different.

Morgan sat by the window and looked out at the people, lights, cars, and noise. As she looked to the crowded street below, she thought of a warm summer night in Beach Lake where her mother was safely asleep. If two cars came down the road in one night, it was a traffic jam. Many people sat on their porch, chatted with neighbors and children's laughter and song could be heard from all directions, she could picture it all so vividly, still relive details in her mind.

On a Sunday morning, the church bells rang and everyone gathered for service, and afterwards people gathered for family dinners. As a young child, Morgan discovered and understood it was the town social day. The day a close knit community would come together, ask about the ill, see newborn babies for the first time and hold their families close. It was a way of life for Morgan. It was an era in time that seemed to remain still and untainted by the growth going on around it. Preserved with some sort of magic dust that made it remain a place to truly grow up and live the rest of your life, numerous generations were ensured safe, secure homes.

It was a different time and place. It was a different life, one she hadn't been able to hold onto, it wasn't hers to keep. As she looked out to the busy street below, out of the window of her lonely Minneapolis condo hundreds of miles from Beach Lake, she would almost swear it all happened to someone else. Someone far, far away she once knew.

Morgan couldn't stop the thoughts, she didn't want to remember things, didn't want to relive days that were long gone. All she wanted was to move forward and erase it all, but that was not to be. Her mind and desires weren't working together and her mind took her to places, her mind took her back. She remembered a warm summer night when she was almost thirteen years old. Morgan, her identical twin sister May, and Ryder had been enjoying ice cream scooped into half a cantaloupe as May spent an hour showing them the purses she'd made with her sewing machine that day. Ryder sat through it as patiently as he could, rolled his eyes to Morgan only when May wasn't looking, and he sighed deeply when she finally gathered her purses and left.

"Why didn't you say anything? Why didn't you tell her you'd look at them later? You just wanted to make me suffer through that." His words accused Morgan and she laughed.

"If I had to sit through it, I didn't see any reason you should be let off."

"You two look like the exact same people, but you're so totally not. And don't you tell any of my friends I sat here and looked at purses for an hour."

"I'm telling them all. I think you liked the yellow one with the feathers on top." Morgan teased and lay back on the ground as she looked up through the branches of the tree to see daylight glisten through in spots.

"I'm glad you're not into all that stuff. How come you're not?"

"That's a stupid question, how do I know?"

"You're identical twins, it's odd she's so into all the girly things and you like ball and stuff."

It was the reason Morgan spent quite a bit of time with Ryder, the boy next door. She loved May, but their differences were many when it came to what interested them, they were so opposite in what they liked to do. Over time, she had tried to get her sister more interested in things she liked to do, and May did the same, and they'd never really met in the middle so their interests remained opposite one another. Having the two people as best friends, May and Ryder, was a nice balance for Morgan, she was lucky to have them both.

Alone now, the two sat underneath the large oak that was immense in proportions and Ryder produced from his pocket a butter knife and began scraping on the tree.

"What are you doing?" Morgan asked with confusion.

"I'm putting our names here, our initials. RM and MB."

"That's stupid."

He looked at her and shook his head with a frustrated look. "Why is everything *stupid* to you? It's your favorite word, *that's stupid, that's stupid,* that's all you say about anything."

"Only the stupid things, and that's stupid. Why are you putting our names like that?"

"Marry me Morgan Bailey." Ryder said with all the gumption of a confident young teen.

"What?" She shouted at him as if the thought were preposterous.

"Marry me. Not now, we're too young, but later. We'll get married and live here in Beach Lake, this is where I want to raise our children." He spoke with such maturity, stared at her and spoke with an assured confidence there was no question what their destiny was.

"I'm not marrying you, Ryder Mason, and I certainly don't want any of your children."

"Why not?" He looked so offended, as if she'd slapped him.

"Because."

"You have to have a reason."

"Then it's because you don't like cats," she huffed, it was the only thing she could think of as she snatched the butter knife out of his hands.

"I never said I didn't like cats."

"But you don't."

"How do you know?" He faced her with a demanding tone.

"You wouldn't get Mrs. Green's cat out of the tree."

"This tree?" He looked up to the massive growth above him then threw his hands in the air and spoke with an exasperated tone. "I like cats, but I would have killed myself. This tree must be a hundred feet high at least, and the cat was ninety nine feet up there. It's the oldest and biggest tree in town."

"Chicken." Morgan scrunched her face at him.

"You want me to climb this tree? I'll climb this dang tree." His ego had been wounded and Ryder began at the base of the tree and started making his way up.

"You're going to kill yourself, don't climb this tree."

"That's why I told you I didn't climb it to begin with because I could kill myself, but if this is what it takes to prove myself to you." Ryder didn't listen to her pleas for him to stop, instead he began climbing with a determination, refused to return to safe ground.

"You don't have to prove yourself." Morgan's nervousness increased the higher he went. "I wouldn't marry you anyway, and it isn't because you don't like cats."

"Then why?"

"It's because you're stupid."

"A stupid, chicken, cat hater. Anything else you want to call me?"

"What I'm going to call is your mother, I'm going to call your mother, Ryder, she told you we're not supposed to climb this tree."

He didn't listen to her as he pushed himself further and further up the huge oak that was giant in size, massive in proportions, and all Morgan could do was watch him as the sun began to fade and the night grew to dusk.

"Ryder, you're far enough, come down now."

When he couldn't seem to get any further, and Morgan continued to insist with urgent pleas, he began his descent down again. One little mishap, one small glitch, and he found himself in a precarious, embarrassing, position. Ryder was situated on a branch and had to swing down to another, but the pant leg of his thin shorts got stuck on a protruding limb, ripped wide open, and he was left dangling in his underwear.

Morgan's scream of fear as she thought he would surely fall straight to his death, called the attention of her mother who called the fire department and they came with several engines with lights flashing and alarms blaring. All the neighbors gathered around on that slow summer evening to see what the fuss was about. As if that wasn't humiliating enough, the news got hold of it and they too showed up with their cameras. Night had fallen and spot lights had to be pointed upwards and they shined bright in the dark sky, highlighted Ryder dangling in his underwear. The light helped get footage for the late night news and pictures from reporters as they too gathered with their equipment.

Using a tall bucket truck that was raised to the great height it needed to be, Ryder was extracted from the tree as everyone watched the progress and when he shifted once and almost fell head first to a sure death, the massive audience that had grown in size until almost the entire town was present, gasped in horror. It was a loud collective sound as the intake of breaths were one of fear, and Morgan's heart jolted so badly she thought she would need the help of medical equipment on standby to get it started again. Finally, after a few hours, he was carefully placed inside the raised bucket then lowered back to safety after being covered with a blanket.

"Ryder, what are you doing up that tree half naked?" His mother scorned him.

"I didn't go up there half naked."

"What are you doing up that tree to begin with?"

He looked over to Morgan. "I had to prove something stupid."

"Something stupid is right. You could have broken every bone in your body if you'd fallen, you could have killed yourself, have you no sense?"

His mother was both relieved he was safe and furious at the same time. Ryder was immediately punished and placed on restriction, but later that night in the wee hours just after midnight, Morgan left her own house, climbed the fence and snuck through the small patch of woods. Then she easily scaled the garage using the trellis and slipped into his always open window and into his room.

"Stupid, I told you it was stupid," Morgan whispered loudly beside his head, jarred him awake and then plopped in next to him.

"You're stupid," he mumbled with sleep.

"I'm not the one on restriction, and I wasn't the one on the late news hanging in my underwear."

Ryder moaned and covered his face with the pillow. "Beach Lake finally had something happen to make the news, and it had to be me dangling upside down in my underwear."

"I can't wait to see the paper tomorrow when I deliver it, maybe you'll be on the front page, not only was the evening news there, there were also reporters with cameras."

She laughed and he joined her, they had to press their faces into the pillow for a long time so as not to be heard, then they finally released it and breathed deep to catch their breaths. The room was quiet when Ryder spoke again.

"I don't care that I was dangling in my underwear, I proved what I needed to prove."

"You proved you're a fool, nothing but one stupid fool Ryder Mason, that's what..."

His voice held the same sure conviction he'd used before, there was no question in his strong statement, it was almost a demand. "Fool or not, you'll marry me one day Morgan Bailey."

Morgan slapped him with a pillow. "Shut up, Ryder."

Through elementary, middle and high school, they were together. Through broken bones and broken noses, birthday parties with cake fights and school dances that ended with making out in the front seat of the car. Then separate colleges came where they discovered the inability to function without the other and Ryder transferred, it was the only way they made it through medical school.

After they graduated and were just beginning their careers as doctors, on a warm summer night, Ryder took her out back to the old oak tree. The early evening was crisp as the setting sun filtered through the leaves and cast a soft glow everywhere. Ryder pointed out the initials of them that he'd made so huge you could see them from across the yard.

"Remember the night I started carving this?" He placed his hand upon the bare spot of wood and traced some of it with his palm.

"The night Beach Lake made the news?" Morgan laughed. "It took you months to finish."

"It didn't help that you kept hiding my knife and I had to steal another from the kitchen."

"I fought you every step of the way." She stepped closer to him and pressed her body to his. Her arms were around him in an instant, she felt so fulfilled just by the touch of him, he made her whole.

"You tried to fight me every step of the way and it worked until the first time we made out, right underneath this tree."

"You took advantage, I was young."

"You were old enough to know you loved me."

Morgan playfully raised her eyebrows. "Did I love you?"

"You always have, you just didn't want to admit it then."

"I can't remember it happening. Do you?"

"It happened before we were born. We're two souls that had no choice but to come together, just happened to be our luck we'd be neighbors." Ryder kissed her tenderly, believed his words to the very core of his being. "So it didn't matter how long you fought it, you would have ended up here with me in the long run, whether you liked it or not."

"You're a good kisser, that's my downfall." She kissed him again, pressed herself even closer, always had to get closer. "And you're a doctor now and that makes you even harder to resist. You've grown into quite a man."

"Well, Dr. Bailey, you're pretty irresistible yourself. Congratulations on your new title by the way."

She laughed, "You too, Dr. Mason."

"Mason and Bailey. That's all we'll need on our little sign over the door."

"With just a slight change, I think it should be Bailey and Mason. Why should you come first?"

Ryder looked to deep blue eyes, looked into her soul that was his lifeline. "We should simplify it, and I have the solution, maybe we should use one name."

"And whose would that be?"

"When I was a young fool, I asked you to marry me once, right here in this spot, right underneath this tree. You called me a stupid, chicken, cat hater. I climbed the tree to prove myself to you and I'd be willing to do it again if I need to. I think my mistake was that I demanded it back then." Ryder got down on one knee and produced a box, when he opened it he revealed his offering of a magnificent, simple, brilliant diamond. "I'm a little older now and a little wiser. This time I'm presenting you with a diamond, I'm down on one knee, and I'm asking instead of demanding. Marry me, Morgan Bailey?"

Morgan's tears were instant, silent tears that flowed down her cheeks as he waited on bended knee. Ryder offered her the world, all she would ever need, and she too got down on her knees on the dirty ground. They kneeled underneath the biggest, oldest and strongest oak in town, but it wasn't nearly as strong as the lifelong bond between them.

"Ryder Mason, how could you ask me such a question? How dare you think you would have any other option?"

When they went back inside to share the news with the others, both their mothers cried and their fathers beamed proud.

"It was expected of course, we've always known you two were on this path, but even that doesn't change how excited I am that it's official." Henry hugged his daughter tight. "I will officially, finally, have my son in my family."

Henry then shook Ryder's hand tight then pulled him in for a hug. "You've always been a son to me, if she had even tried to get away and marry someone else you know that wouldn't have happened."

Ryder laughed. "I was pretty confident you had my back, Mr. Bailey."

Henry huffed and waved his hand. "I've been telling you for years not to call me that, don't you think it's about time you listened to me."

"Okay, Dad." He said it with hesitation and looked to his own father across the room who smiled in approval.

Both Bea and Ryder's mother began chatting with joyous excitement about the plans to be made, invitations, the church, flowers, details to be worked out, but ideas filled the room immediately.

"A date, we need a date." Bea said and the entire room looked to Ryder and Morgan.

"Today? Tomorrow?" Ryder teased and pulled Morgan close.

May spoke up then. "I'll need at least six months to design the dress, I could probably do it in less time, but give me six months."

Morgan looked to her twin sister she had confidence in, it wasn't a question of whether she would want her sister to design her dress, it was a little surprise she would take on the task. "You're going to design it?"

"Design it and make it. It has to be the most magnificent thing anyone has ever seen, I know I'm going to use the pearls and lace from Mama's dress, and..." Then May paused as the room had become quiet. "And I'm not going to tell you or anyone else a thing."

"I'm supposed to trust you?"

"Of course you are." May smiled with confidence and without question in her face or voice.

Morgan was about to protest then looked to Ryder. "I don't care what I walk down the aisle in, it will never matter as long as he'll be at the end of it."

He pulled her into him closer still. "I've waited my entire lifetime for this, I guess I can wait at least six months longer, but it isn't going to be a long aisle, the shorter the better."

Their lives unfolded before them as if it was a story already written and one simply turned the pages. Plans were made and childhood dreams took shape to become reality as they looked for a house to purchase in Beach Lake, one to live in after the wedding, raise their children and have their own medical practice together.

In those moments of true bliss, no one could possibly know that things would go so terribly wrong. In their worst nightmare, there wasn't a person that could have guessed the direction their lives would take or that it would be so drastically altered. No one could have possibly prepared themselves for what unfolded soon after.

****

"Hey beautiful," Ryder kissed her tenderly on the neck as she stood over the sink. "How's my bride to be?"

"Frustrated. The florist called today and they're having trouble finding the flowers I wanted."

"We don't have to have any flowers at all. Nothing but you and me, that's all that has to be there."

"That's probably all that will be there. There's no one in town who wants to be there now."

"Morgan, there isn't a person in Beach Lake who would forgive us if they weren't, they've watched us fall in love over the years and they've been looking forward to this day as long as we have."

"Well, that was before…"

He waited but she didn't finish, Morgan wouldn't say the words. Instead, she tried to push her feelings aside, never wanted to acknowledge openly what happened, not with specific words. If she ignored it, maybe she could avoid reality. Saying words out loud meant that it had actually happened, it had all been real, and she wasn't ready to come to terms with that so she avoided talking about it.

Morgan let it smolder and burn inside, a dangerous festering of her pain. When he turned her around he could see from her eyes it had been another difficult day. He touched her cheek gently. "How was your day?"

"It was another day," she smiled but it was forced as she changed the subject. "I made soup."

"I was going to take you out tonight. You are staying tonight, aren't you?" She'd stayed with him in his apartment in the city since the accident, but he wasn't sure day to day if she'd be there when he got home or not, wasn't sure of anything anymore.

"Staying? Where else am I going to go?"

"Not that I don't want you here, but you can go home, Morgan."

"No I can't." She stated quickly and turned back around to the sink, ready to absorb herself in something else again.

Ryder pressed himself to her and held her close to stop her from avoiding him. "Maybe you should, I'll go with you. You don't have to stay there, but maybe if we take it slow."

"Ryder, I can't."

He knew she didn't want to talk of it, she never did. As usual, she would let her anxiety take hold and bury it deep somewhere so she wouldn't have to deal with it. She went on day to day in a quiet torment no matter what he did to try and help her. Ryder wasn't sure when she would deal with what happened because she kept pushing it further and further away and by her avoiding it, it made it so much harder to get through.

"Was today better or worse than yesterday?" He asked.

"I told you, it was another day and it's over." She sighed and turned back around to face him again and let him hold her. Morgan felt the comfort he offered but she only wished it could ease all her suffering. The day was coming to a close and she wasn't looking forward to another dark night and it was fast approaching.

"Let's talk about it."

"I did, I said it was over, just another day, Ryder, nothing special."

"Not this day specifically, you know we need to talk about the accident."

Her face changed to an angry hardness, a façade she used to block him. "Do you have to start as soon as you walk in?"

"It doesn't matter when I bring it up, you still won't talk about it. Is an hour from now better? Maybe in the morning? I can wait, but we need to talk about it."

"What is there to talk about, it happened, I..."

"You what? Say it Morgan, tell me what you're thinking?" He stressed and tried to hold her but she pulled away and left for the other room as if she could escape it.

"I don't want to talk about it."

"You had a horrible day, you don't go to work, you don't go out, and your nightmares are getting worse. I think we should see Dr. Diaz." He was hesitant to bring up the subject again when she was resistant to the suggestion every time he mentioned it.

"We? You mean me. It doesn't bother you, you just go to work day after day like nothing happened."

"I'm trying to get past this, I'm trying to help you get past this."

"And it's easy for you, isn't it? I'm the only one who..." She stopped herself and wouldn't elaborate further.

"Don't push me out, talk to me. And don't think you're the only one going through this, we're all trying to deal with what's happened." She couldn't see she wasn't alone in this and he stopped himself from getting quickly frustrated. She wouldn't seek out the help she needed, more help than he seemed to be able to give her on his own, Morgan needed professional help but she wouldn't consider it a possibility. She refused to entertain the thought yet she seemed to be getting worse day after day.

"Maybe I don't want to get past it, maybe I don't want to let them go."

"Just because you get past it doesn't mean you let them go, it doesn't mean you forget all about them. You have to grieve, you haven't even cried except in your sleep."

"So all I need is a good cry?" She spat sarcastically. "That's going to solve all my problems?"

"Morgan, I'm not the enemy here, I don't want to fight with you." He took her back in his arms, knew the anger would take hold and she'd be miserable for the rest of the night. It's what she did. "Don't do this, Morgan, we need to talk to someone."

"A good cry and a psychiatrist, that's your solution."

"I wish I had the solution, but would it hurt to try?"

"Everything hurts, Ryder." Her voice was soft and childlike as she sighed and leaned into him, let him hold her once more.

"I know baby," he said tenderly as he stroked her back to soothe her as best he could. His voice was a whisper that emulated her pain. "I know."

There wasn't much he could do for her, there wasn't much she would let him do. He couldn't force her to talk about it to him or anyone else, he could only be there for her as much as she would let him, hold her night after night as her nightmares progressed. In a fetal position she would cry out in her pain, and he would suffer his own alone. The agony of what they'd lost, and the agony of feeling as if he was losing her too tortured him yet he was strong because she needed him to be.

Every night before she fell asleep he'd whisper to her something from their long ago childhood, only as a child, he hadn't known how important the simple intention of the words would become. There was more meaning to them now, something he sincerely prayed for as she whimpered in her agony after sleep came.

"Sweet dreams, Morgan, until tomorrow."

But there came a morning that Morgan was no longer there. One night as he lay sleeping, she didn't take anything when she silently closed the door behind her when she left.

****

After four years, she would have thought the memories wouldn't have been in such clear detail, would have thought they would have faded by now. Morgan could still see faces and hear voices as if they stood right next to her. At times she was successful in blocking it all out, suppressing her thoughts of the past, but she was having difficulty with that task lately.

When would it stop? When would it all truly go away and leave her? Morgan had been so lost in her thoughts of the past she hadn't heard her pager going off, finally felt it vibrate against her and looked to the number to see it was the hospital. She was grateful for the interruption.

CHAPTER TWO

"You are fantastically on schedule to give birth soon. Everything looks great and couldn't be better." Morgan smiled but the woman before her looked as if she still had reservations. "It was a false alarm and I assure you, everything is fine."

"I think I'm glad it was a false alarm, I don't think I'm ready. I guess scared like every other new mother. It's so easy to take care of this baby while it's in my stomach Dr. Bailey, I just worry about when she gets out."

Morgan raised her eyebrows. "She?"

"I have this strong intuition it's a girl. I've been calling her Meagan for months. I hope if I'm wrong and it's a boy, he won't hold it against me."

Morgan saw it many times. A mother's intuition of what the gender was and more often than not they were right, and if she'd done an official study she'd find the percentages were higher they were correct. She once wondered that if they were wrong, if the child grew up with gender confusion at being called Anna for nine months and end up with a name like Bob.

"I can't give you an instruction book, but don't be scared, you'll be a great mom. You'll know what to do." Morgan tried to quench her fears and apprehensions and the woman smiled, a little nervousness gone. She saw it in many of her patients the closer the time to delivery. "If I don't see you in the hospital in labor before then, I'll see you next week for your scheduled appointment."

"We'll both be here in one form or another, me and Meagan May Stampler."

Her words were said cheerily and Morgan's heart stopped. She stood with a strange expression at the name, her look cause for concern again from her patient.

"You don't like the name?"

"It's... I..." Breathe Morgan, just breathe. It was a name. "It's lovely, my sister's name was May."

"Oh." The woman's smile was broad at the news, but she still saw something odd on her doctor's face, then she realized she said 'was'. And Dr. Bailey didn't look like she was going to elaborate and give any more information than that.

Morgan seemed to get past it and smiled. "I think it's a great name, again, I just hope if it's a son he won't mind it so much."

When she left the room she stood silently outside the door a few minutes to pull herself together, and then pushed it, forced it, to the way back recesses of her mind. It was early morning now and there was no need to go back home and try to sleep so she went to her office to begin her appointments. There was a lax period of time in the early afternoon when she caught a quick power nap, it was always easier for her to sleep during the day and the nap was enough to get her through the rest of the day with ease.

It looked to be a quiet night and with the emergency call she'd spent all night in the hospital for, and her long day, it would probably be enough to make her sleep well that night. It wasn't guaranteed, sleep eluded her most times, but she held out hope as she finished her day and headed for home.

Morgan had just stepped out the door of her office building when Nancy, her best friend, just stepped from a cab.

"I was going to surprise you." Nancy said as she hugged her. "Ray's at the hospital across town and I'm going home with him but not until later. I thought we could grab dinner since I was here and you probably haven't eaten, you never do."

"I wish you'd have called, it's been a long day." Morgan's thoughts were still on the mention of May's name, it was foolish for it to have an effect on her but she couldn't shake it. She wasn't in the mood for dinner and said so. "I'm really exhausted, Nancy, maybe we could…"

"Nonsense, I'm here now and we won't be late. What are you going to do? Go home to that empty apartment of yours and a carton of ice cream for dinner?"

"Something with chocolate and brownies."

"I'm saving you, you don't have anything else to do." Nancy grabbed her arm and drug her down the sidewalk.

"Do you have to make my life sound so pathetic?" Morgan asked with a smile. It was pathetic and Nancy didn't need to remind her.

"I have to wait for Ray and he'll be another few hours. Come on, we'll go over to that little quiet Italian place around the corner. You'll be saving me from a load of paperwork, and if you're not hungry at least a glass of wine."

Nancy was a dear friend and colleague she'd worked with until her and her husband picked up their family and moved to the suburbs to begin a small family practice. She never faltered to ask how happy she still was with the partnership Morgan worked, and that evening was no exception.

"I always have to ask, are you ready yet or still happy there?" Nancy inquired.

"Still happy. Had you opened your practice in the city I might have second thoughts, but the country is too quiet for me."

"You like the hustle, you like having no life. If you moved to the suburbs with us you might find one there." Nancy saw her friend's life as a lonely one but there'd been nothing she did that was successful in changing it. Morgan didn't see a need for change.

"There you go again, making my life sound pathetic. Not all of us are cut out for the white picket fence and rose garden. I like the city."

"And you'd love the country and the small town life. It's what you came from, isn't it? Beach Lake is one of those towns."

Morgan wanted to react somehow but didn't as she sat still. There it was again, something from her past at the most unexpected time. What was forcing it all to the forefront? Why were things coming at her from every angle? Haunts from another life that seemed to come from nowhere and assault her senses when she least saw it coming. She didn't scream, nor did she look fazed in the least at the mention of her hometown.

"Maybe that's why I'm not there anymore." It was so much more than that, but Morgan had never revealed that to Nancy or anyone else. No one knew much of her background or where she'd come from before she began her life there.

"So you've had a taste of the city, isn't that what you've been doing? Living in a small town all your life and you've now had a taste of the city. Haven't you had your fill yet?" Nancy ordered a bottle of wine and a huge plate of pasta to share. If she hadn't, Morgan wouldn't have eaten a thing.

"You'll be the first to know when I'm tired of the city."

Nancy looked to Morgan and would have thought that would be the day she was ready for something else. She could see something very unhappy about Morgan and it didn't sit well. "So what's wrong today?"

Morgan looked at her, tried to smile but it looked forced. "Nothing, just a long day."

"And? You look like... I don't know, like it's something else."

"It isn't anything that a good night's sleep won't cure."

"You'd get sleep in the country. It's quiet, it's..."

"Nancy." Morgan sighed and interrupted her. "I'm not moving, end of discussion."

"Until another day then, but the conversation isn't over."

"You're relentless, will you never give up?"

"One of these days I'm going to catch you on the right day. If you don't want to talk about moving, why don't we talk about a trip out of town? Ray has a conference to go to and I was going to meet him afterwards to get away for a few days, want to come?"

"That sounds great. Me, you and your lovely husband," she said it sarcastically. "A romantic weekend for three."

"You know he'd love to have you."

"And I know he'd love it better if he had alone time with his wife."

"It's at a great resort that serves marvelous frozen drinks. Doesn't that at least appeal to you?"

"I have too much going on right now. How are the kids?" Morgan questioned.

"Flourishing in the country." She tried to rub it in and make it sound good, knew it would go ignored. "The kids are having the grandest time being able to walk outside the front door and play in the yard instead of all of us having to take a cab to the nearest park. And Ray actually bought a mini-van, said it was mandatory."

Morgan sipped her wine. "Surely you didn't give up your two-seater sports job."

"We have too much fun in that to give it up. It sits in the garage quite a bit, but we get out on occasion. What about you? What have you been doing for fun since I'm not here to make sure you have any?"

"No time for that."

"Dr. Driswell told me you added more patients. If you want my opinion, that's the last thing you needed. You're already overworked, what did you need more for?" Nancy questioned her but knew she wouldn't get an answer. She often suspected there was something Morgan was running from, something buried deep she'd yet to reveal to her best friend if she ever would. "You're overworked and need a break, come with me."

"Why don't I watch the kids instead?" That was something Morgan could look forward to, maybe it would help take her mind off things, and Nancy's girls, Emily and Amy, would be good distraction.

"It would be even more perfect if you came with us. Evan is going to the conference too, he can stay afterwards. It will be fun, the four of us for a few days."

Morgan smiled to herself, Nancy took it as she smiled about Evan and that was fine. Nancy and Ray had set the two of them up on a blind date and they continued to let them think there was a relationship between them. They were nothing but friends, Evan in love with his ex wife still and Morgan not interested, but the illusion of them being involved with one another had kept the two potential matchmakers at bay. They didn't lie about anything they just revealed very little and both Nancy and Ray always read more into it.

"Evan told me he was going and looking forward to some golf, but I'd prefer to stay with the kids. Afterwards, you and Ray have a nice time and Evan can come over to the house and keep me company." Morgan didn't lie, she'd mention it to him and he would stop in and see her she was sure, and Nancy and Ray could think what they wanted.

"You don't have to stay with the kids, they're staying with friends, but you would be their first preference."

"They'd give up a weekend at a friend's house for me?"

"They'd give up living at a friend's house for you. It isn't only Ray and I that want you to move out there, they ask me about it all the time. They miss having you around all the time."

"I miss them too." Morgan often spent her spare time with them, the highlight of her life it seemed.

"See, another reason…"

"Stop, don't say it," she laughed. "I see them often enough. They'll get to an age soon where they'll tire of me anyway. Emily is getting close, she's a teenager now, I imagine hanging out with an old woman like me won't be on her priority list soon."

"I think if I disappeared they wouldn't even notice as long as you were still around."

Morgan picked at the food. "I do miss them, you didn't have to move so far away."

"It's an hour and a half drive, sometimes it takes that long to get two blocks in the city," Nancy smiled, "Besides, Evan is there too. We're there, he's there, what else is left in the city for you?"

Morgan thought about her question and knew there was nothing in the city for her, but there was nothing in the suburbs either. No matter where she was, the heartbreak and pain would be the same. It didn't have anything to do with her physical presence or where she was, then again, it had everything to do with where she was. She wasn't home and could never go home again.

"Why is it that every time we get together the conversation centers on my life?" Morgan asked, wanted to change the subject.

"Because you need a life."

"I have a life thank you."

"You're a wonderful doctor, Morgan, but you're also a beautiful single woman. I want you to be happy, I care about you."

"And you think the fresh air of the country and a walk down a small little town main street is the kind of life I need. I'm happy for you, I really am, but that is you and Ray, it isn't me."

"I have hopes that if I can't talk you into it, Evan can. Ray is so excited you two are getting along so well. I think he already has patients lined up for you both when you join our practice."

Morgan laughed, laughed more to the shock they would be in when they one day discovered that the two of them were nothing more than friends and never would be. Morgan and Evan's devised plan had worked so well, they were so happy about it, but she knew they would be devastated when the truth was discovered.

Ray and Nancy had placed the two as an item the first night Ray had set them up on a blind date. Plans were a dinner with him and Nancy at their house when Morgan made an escape while they were in the kitchen and she drug Evan along with her. He was handsome, a very nice man, but she knew instinctively after asking about divorce that he was still in love with his ex wife. Each of them agreed that their relationship wouldn't go anywhere, but didn't tell the two matchmakers any specifics and remained friends. It was a relationship they enjoyed and it kept them off both their backs to think the two were a successful pairing.

The first night they escaped, they'd driven to a small restaurant and had a great dinner. With no uncomfortable feelings of a 'date' between them, each relaxed and the conversation flowed easily. Evan talked of his wife and divorce. She couldn't take the late nights and him never being home and being on call at all hours, working most weekends, it was the typical doctor's life that forced him into separation then divorce.

"I think that's why Ray and Nancy work so well, they're both doctor's." Morgan had said.

"They are a rare find."

"But they have their flaws, they like to think everyone can find what they have."

"And we can at least give the impression that we have. I have to say this idea of yours was great. The last time Ray tried to set me up, the woman came dressed in black leather and chains, he didn't know her side job from being a nurse at the hospital was, well, she thought it was a business arrangement."

Morgan laughed until her face hurt. "You've got to be kidding. You think that would have taught him a thing or two."

"He's definitely more careful now. You're the first set up since that one, so I was a little scared to say the least, but I'm having a better time than I thought I would and I don't have to worry about calling you tomorrow."

"Hey, I never said anything about not calling me." Morgan said.

"Should I say, I don't feel obligated to call you, there's a difference."

Morgan smiled. "I've had a good time also. Call me when you're in the city and we'll do something."

"I'm in a few times a month."

"Good. That's about all the time I could muster up, a few times a month."

They even danced afterwards at the adjacent club then left only because they were closing for the night, both disappointed when it was time to go. When Evan pulled up to the house it was dark except for the porch light.

"Think they're really mad at us?" He asked.

Morgan laughed. "Probably peeking out of the window like they were waiting for their teenager to come home, maybe we should breathe hard and fog up the windows."

"You're hell bent on getting them off your trail, aren't you?"

She sighed. "You just don't know."

"What are you going to tell them? What am I supposed to tell Ray when he asks?"

Morgan thought about it. "We don't have to lie, just be nonchalant about it, mysterious, they won't ask specific details. Just tell him you enjoyed my company and you're going to call me, that won't be a lie."

"And when I do call you, and we get together in the city, I'll tell him we did."

"See? It will work perfect. Let them read into it what they will."

"Maybe I should walk you to the door."

"No, if they are peeking they'd expect you to kiss me." Morgan looked to the house, was sure Nancy was in one of the windows. "We'll let them guess at what we're doing in the car."

As time passed the plan worked to perfection, and sometimes Morgan felt almost guilty Ray was so excited, but they'd done nothing to instigate it. They saw each other for lunch, sometimes dinner, or a quick cup of coffee on occasion when Evan was in the city, even managed an entire day or two of visiting museums or going to the movies without interruption. But they were friends, and that's all they would remain no matter how badly Ray or Nancy wished otherwise. It was just easier to let them think what they did, if not, they would be searching for others to set them up with.

As she and Nancy lingered over a cup of coffee that night, her friend wanted to know how Evan was and how things were going. Morgan told her without lying what they'd been up to, they'd just had dinner recently or met for coffee at the hospital.

"I knew you two would work." Nancy smiled proud and excited. "I know it's just a matter of time you'll be in the country but I have a hard time being patient."

"I know you mean well, but just be my friend, Nancy, not my life guide." Morgan faced her squarely. "Quit worrying about me so much. I'll have time for another life one day, but I'm too busy with this one right now. You'll be the first to know if anything changes."

Morgan knew she would find nothing in the suburbs in the way of a life. There would only be the same emptiness the city offered, the same emptiness she was destined to carry with her everywhere no matter where she was. Besides, the kind of life Nancy had with her husband in the suburbs was so close in comparison to what she once dreamed for herself, she knew it would only make it more difficult to be in someone else's dream when her own had been stolen by a horrid twist of fate.

****

Morgan's mother had called and left several more messages and she tried to reach her a few times but her mother refused to have an answering machine. Most times when she thought of it, it was too late in the evening and she wasn't concerned, the messages hadn't sounded urgent, but she began to wonder about her persistence.

Morgan was sitting in her office and had just hung up from another attempt when her assistant rang in to tell her Ray was on the line.

"Not you too," Morgan said as soon as she picked up the phone, knowing the reason for his call.

"Me what?" He said with feigned innocence.

"You're calling to see if I'm going to the conference, aren't you?"

"I told Nancy I'd give it one final shot, and you know I have to do what she says or she has my hide."

"I'm beginning to think all of you stay up late at night to conspire against me, you time yourselves that just when I don't think you're going to try anymore, one of you mentions it."

"It'll be fun."

"I'll tell you what I tell Nancy and Evan, send me a postcard. I really can't go, I have an associate out of town and I have his patients as well as mine." Morgan looked to the new stack of folders on her desk. They were piled on top of the conference schedule she hadn't even opened and looked at. Had she done so, she would have seen a very familiar name as a guest speaker.

"I tried. I have to say though, as much as I want you to come, the girls would never speak to me again if I had managed to talk you into it."

"See how things work out? You'll have a great time playing golf and spending time with your beautiful wife, and I'll get my break playing a kid."

"I guess it's a mute point to say not too much pizza and soda." He laughed, knew she would spoil them. "You know how Nancy is about eating the good stuff now, but the girls know where all the restaurant take-out phone numbers are." He wouldn't come out and admit he'd used the numbers himself. "So if I can't talk you into it, at least I know you'll be having fun."

Morgan laughed and shook her head when she hung up the phone, pictured Ray sneaking a pizza or two on occasion with his kids when his wife wasn't looking. She then glanced at the conference schedule underneath her papers and something told her to pull it out, maybe just glance at it for some odd reason. But just as she had her hand on it, her assistant came in with the news she had a patient in labor who'd come to her office instead of going to the hospital.

CHAPTER THREE

Ryder Mason placed the chart on the peg and reached for his jacket. "I'm leaving for the day."

"Where are you going?" The receptionist asked as she was about to hand him another folder for his next patient. "You have Mrs. Jenkins in room three with Tommy, he's got…"

"Dr. Cater is taking that one, I have to go."

"You know how Tommy is, he only likes to see you."

"I've already talked to him, he'll be fine with Dr. Cater today."

The receptionist looked satisfied with his explanation. "At least I won't have to listen to Stella's voice on the phone again." She rolled her eyes and sighed. "She's been calling all day."

"Next time she calls, just tell her I'm gone."

"That isn't where you're going? I thought you were going to meet her. She won't like it, and she'll scream at me."

"She screams at everyone." He sighed and left.

It didn't matter that she would scream, at his assistant, at him when she couldn't reach him and didn't know where he was, Ryder didn't care, and he didn't much care what she did and wished she'd get the hint and leave, but she stuck around and he never had the energy or inclination to change the situation. It was harder for him to take the time for a messy breakup than it was to simply go along with it.

As his car drove out of the city he turned his cell phone off and looked forward to the silence of the drive. When he first began his career and had to live in the city, he used to feel so different when he drove the familiar road, used to have something to drive home to because Morgan would be waiting for him there. Now, it was as if he was going to visit and he didn't like the feeling.

Beach Lake was his home, where he grew up, fell in love, and planned his life. His dreams were destroyed and shattered now like dust he'd held in his hand and watched the wind blow it all away. And although it should have been long enough, at times it was still difficult to face, and this would be one of those times.

He would be visiting Bea and would have to go into the house. Ryder often thought that it would have gotten much easier over time but it still pained him, sometimes not so bad, but sometimes it unnerved him. Now would be one of those unsettling times, especially since Morgan had been on his mind at a constant rate lately, and he wasn't sure why.

Ryder tried, tried desperately not to think anymore, not to feel anymore, to push it aside. He even tried to tell himself Stella was what he needed, but the more time he spent with her, the more time he wanted to spend away from her. If he just allowed himself to let it go maybe there would be hope, but just when he thought he was on the verge of it something struck him.

He had come across an old college t-shirt of Morgan's the other day in a drawer, or hear a song on the radio, a song they'd danced to. It was so bad one night a few weeks ago he almost thought he could hear her breathing beside him, even physically found himself subconsciously reaching over to feel her next to him, only to find cold space. The emptiness would overwhelm him then, and the void in his heart and soul would begin to throb like a physical agony. He just wanted to forget, it was all he wanted, but Morgan couldn't be erased, she was still so much an emotional part of his life and he suspected would always be.

When Ryder arrived, he didn't go to the front door, never did, he went around to the back and walked right in. When he let go of the screen as he stepped onto the porch, it slammed shut with a creak and a bang, echoed out in the quiet night.

"Ryder," Bea smiled broadly from the stove when he stepped inside. She wiped her hands quickly and gave him a warm hug, her usual greeting. "I'm glad you could come. I hope I didn't interrupt anything you had planned."

"I've told you time and again you don't interrupt anything. You're always first Bea, everything else has to worry about interrupting you." He stepped inside the familiar house as the smell of a home cooked dinner wafted through the air. This was one of those times he would suffer through, but he smiled as if it didn't bother him.

She'd made his favorite, traditional pot roast with fresh mashed potatoes and lot's of gravy to go along with it. There was also a large basket of fresh, out of the oven, homemade rolls.

"Who else is coming?" He laughed as he picked up the lid of a pot and looked at the enormous amount of mashed potatoes. "Are you expecting a football team?"

"I know, I used a whole bag of potatoes, its habit and I still can't get the hang of cooking in small portions." She almost looked embarrassed as she made the admission. "Foolish, isn't it? I'm used to huge meals as if a family…" Then she stopped and wiped her hands on the dishtowel. "Oh well, it won't go to waste, you can take it with you when you leave, I'll never eat this much food."

They talked of many things as they sat and enjoyed the meal together. His parents who he'd visited with briefly before coming to her house, they informed him they were going away on a two week vacation soon. They'd been traveling quite a bit now, enjoying their retired life and liked that one of his brothers and one sister lived out of town and it was someplace to visit. They also talked of his other siblings, nieces and nephews, then a little of his work. Bea didn't have family to talk about, they'd been lost to the both of them.

"How's the city life?"

"It's a life," he said, and then he tried to make it sound better than it was, added more for her benefit. "I think I might buy a new place, I've been renting for quite awhile and it's about time I committed and bought a place. Tired of paying someone else's mortgage."

"You'll buy a place in the city?"

"There's a new condominium development close to my office. The area is really building up, I have more options now and I think it's about time I settled in."

"I just thought..." She was hesitant to say more.

"Thought I might start my own practice here? In Beach Lake?" Ryder asked quietly.

"I always thought you would eventually. If you buy a place, you'll be fully committed there and, and maybe you won't come back either."

"You mean like Morgan?" He had to say it, knew it was what she was thinking.

"She might come back."

"Is that what she said?"

Then Bea felt guilty for giving him hope. "No, it's what I've been hoping for, just my wishes spoken out loud."

"How is she?"

"She's still the same I imagine. She doesn't call much and when I call there seems to be little time for her to talk. She's really busy."

He knew the last words seemed to give her a legitimate reason she didn't talk to Morgan as much as she should. Bea was making excuses for a daughter who had no viable excuse not to keep in touch with a lonely widowed mother. Bea gave her understanding and the benefit of the doubt, but Ryder had developed an angry edge over time.

He didn't want to talk about Morgan so he went back to the subject. "I'm almost set to sign a contract on the new place, when I do and I move in, you can be my first dinner guest. It's a nice place."

Bea smiled with hesitation. "That's great."

"I'll still come and visit Bea. Just because I buy a place doesn't mean I'll be here any less. You and mom are still the only one's who will feed me meals like this. This kind of cooking is a lost art in today's world." He saw she looked hesitant to believe him. "Nothing will change."

"It isn't that. Here I was hoping you'd be moving back to Beach Lake, but I actually wanted to talk to you about me moving out."

Ryder set his fork down and leaned forward, unsure what she was to tell him and she looked unsure about it herself.

It took Bea a few moments to get the words out. "It's been a long time now, and... this house is so big for one person. I think I want to sell it."

He was quiet, the words not something he expected, and he would never expect them but should have known they would come one day. Bea went on as if she needed to explain her reasons to him.

"There's no one but me and as much as I thought it would happen, I have to realize that Morgan won't be coming home."

"Have you talked to her about selling the house?" Ryder was very interested to hear what she would have said about it.

"Not yet. I wanted to talk to you about it first, maybe just to reassure me it's the right thing to do. I don't talk to her much, I can't talk to her. I try, but..." she paused before going on. "It wasn't an easy decision, there's so much here. It's my home. It was... it was so full of life once, but it's so empty now."

He couldn't have agreed with her more. The kitchen once bustled with a vibrant family and he could still picture all of them around the table with May and her father throwing rolls and Morgan hiding the cat on her lap underneath the table, the one he'd gotten her after she accused him of being a cat hater. Bea would have a stove full of food that would seem to be enough to last days but by the time the meal was over, everything would be gone.

Afterwards they would linger, talking and laughing, and sometimes his parents would come over for coffee and dessert if they hadn't been there for dinner. It was as if a party went on all the time, but it wasn't a party, it was life. Life went on inside the walls of this old home and if one was still and listened closely you could still hear the distant sounds of days gone by. Now, only the two of them sat in the immense, empty space. Without words in the air, all that could be heard was the ticking of a distant clock and the occasional barking of a neighbor's dog in the distance, or sometimes a passing car, or the sound of a mother calling a child home. But it was the quiet that reverberated through the empty space as if it were actually an audible sound.

Ryder took her hand across the table. "I know it couldn't have been easy for you to even begin to think about. But I understand Bea, if you think you need approval from me, I understand. I know it's been hard for you here, it's hard for me to come here sometimes, I can only imagine how difficult it is for you, especially being here day in and day out by yourself."

"Henry and May have been gone for so long now, and I can't see Morgan coming back. I've tried but it hasn't done any good. I was going to ask her if she wanted the house first, of course, it is her home too."

Was her home, Ryder wanted to say but didn't. She'd walked away from her home, walked away from him, even walked away from her mother in a time of need, and as much as he tried to understand he found it hard sometimes to forgive her as easily as Bea had. Maybe because she'd taken away his life when she snuck away in the middle of the night, taken his dreams along with her, and never looked back.

"I imagine if she had any intentions of coming back she would have done so by now." Ryder said with that obvious edge to his voice he couldn't keep from slipping out.

When the phone rang Bea rose to answer it and Ryder cleared the few things from the table then stepped out onto the back porch a moment to give her some privacy. He looked out to the backyard where so many things in his life happened. His own yard was directly behind it, he couldn't see the yard itself because of a high wooden fence, but he saw the second floor of his parent's home, the window of his childhood bedroom where he would shine the flashlight out of.

He and Morgan had made up their own signals to communicate in the middle of the night. He never really understood all she'd written down for him to study and get right, he merely flashed the light and they each pretended they were saying something to the other.

Of course that was after a long day of being together anyway and it was still not enough. They'd still be up until after midnight on hot summer evenings, neither one wanted to let go. But they were children then and things changed, she had let go now. After a lifetime together, a lifetime before them that was on the verge of playing out, she'd let go when she left it all behind her.

Ryder hadn't talked to Morgan since the day she called to tell him she was leaving his life forever. A day he tried desperately to get past but he always stumbled and couldn't find his way out. He was quiet, buried in deep memories of the past when Bea stepped out on the porch.

"That was the woman from a place over in Hastings I've been looking at. I have an appointment tomorrow if you want to come with me. I'm not very experienced at this sort of thing." Bea said as she joined him.

Ryder knew she didn't need his permission, but she wanted him there, and he'd be there to walk her through it if it's what she wanted to do. Her life was changing, and as a good son would, just like one she'd given birth to, he would go with her. He wasn't her true son, and Bea may not have given birth to him, but she was as important as his own mother and always would be.

"Of course I'll go with you, Bea."

"I don't know what I'd do without you, I don't..." She was going to say she didn't have anyone else but it was still sad to her that her own daughter had pretty much abandoned her. She too looked out to a backyard that used to be filled with laughter and song now was only dark and silent. It would remain that way until someone else could fill it again.

"I'll help with anything I can help with, you know that."

When he looked across the fence and up to his old bedroom, he pictured Morgan climbing up the trellis and into his always open window. Ryder was taken away in the memory and almost laughed out loud when he thought of the time something had scared her in the middle of the night and she'd run haphazardly through the small patch of woods. She'd crawled through his window looking like a monster, with her hair all out of place and her t-shirt and pants dirty and torn.

"There's something living in the woods," she whispered out of breath. "It's big and hairy."

He laughed at the sight of her. "You look like you wrestled it down, did you win?"

"I'm serious, Ryder, it was huge."

"You probably heard a mouse."

"It wasn't a mouse, it was gigantic." She plopped beside him on the bed as she always did. "It was huge, it was hairy and it had big teeth."

"You could see teeth?"

"Fangs."

The next day after some investigating, they'd discovered a ground hog had made his home there but Morgan swore it was much larger the night before. As she made up a story, she almost convinced him that only the super sized groundhogs came out at night and he almost believed her.

Then he looked to the very spot he'd kissed her for the first time. Right underneath the oak tree after a night of catching lightning bugs, it was just before he hopped onto the fence and over it. He'd done it quickly, afraid she would be angry and he didn't want to stick around to see or hear any reaction. Thought she would have slapped him across the face had he waited. That was the night Ryder discovered he would always have to have Morgan in his life, probably the night he fell in love with her, though at nine, he didn't quite know what love was or how painful it would be.

As he stood in the quiet night with Bea, he recalled many others in his mind as his gaze fixed to the window that was closed and dark now, had been for a long time. Her selling this home would put an end to an era in his life that had shaped him, formed him into the man he was. It would be just as hard for him as it was for Bea, but he would support her in whatever decision she thought was best.

They stood in silence for quite some time before Bea spoke again. Her words trying to convince herself she'd made the right decision. "I can't hang on to it because it needs more than I can give it, just a big old house anyway."

Just a big old house, Ryder said the words over in his mind, just a big old house. If he needed any more encouragement to get on with his life, this was it. Bea selling this house would officially put an end to a day long past, one he couldn't go back to, one that had taken away so many things with it.

As a young boy then as a young man with so much before him, Ryder never would have imagined what had been in store. Never would have imagined standing alone with his dreams scattered about the yard among the dirt and the overgrown garden full of weeds. They'd each lost so much. Although she thought it was best, and wouldn't change her mind, Bea began to cry at so much they'd lost.

"It wasn't supposed to be like this. Nothing like this was ever supposed to happen, it always happened to other people."

Ryder knew where her words came from, he often thought the same. He had gone through it in a trance as if it hadn't happened and all he had to do was wake up, but it wasn't a nightmare he could wake from, wasn't something that happened to someone else, it had happened to him. So he forced a smile on his face for the outside world to see, learned how to laugh and carry on so no one could see what he hid underneath.

What no one could see was the misery and desolation he felt at having his life stolen from him. Like a thief, Morgan had left in the middle of the night and taken it all with her.

CHAPTER FOUR

The chance to spend time with Nancy's kids was what took her through the days until the time came. As much as Nancy looked forward to a few days away with Ray, Morgan looked forward to a few days away from her own responsibilities. She'd been so restless and discontent with everything. Her nightmares had begun again in full force and she couldn't seem to get her mind off her father and sister. So Morgan thought a few active days with Emily who was thirteen and Amy who was six, should be enough to get her back to as normal as she could feel.

With assurances and wishes to have a good time, Nancy drove off to the airport with a smile on her face, one that became even bigger when she saw Evan pull up in the drive.

"Nice timing," Morgan said with a smile as she hugged him in greeting.

"I couldn't have planned it better if I had planned it."

"How was your flight?"

"Great. The plane was a little late getting out, had to wait for a storm to pass, but not too late, so I thought I'd stop by on my way home. Did you just get here?"

"No, I came last night, gave the on call duties to someone else and decided to come early."

"Ray is certainly anxious for Nancy to get there, he's probably waiting for her at the airport now."

Morgan walked into the kitchen and he followed. "I didn't think Nancy was going to make it all day, she actually tried to get an earlier flight, that's why I came last night, just in case she did, but she couldn't. I think this will be the first time they've had a few days alone since Emily was ten."

Evan noticed the empty house as they walked through the living room. "Where are the girls?"

"Emily is at soccer and Amy at a friend's for a little cupcake party."

He sat down in the kitchen chair as she set about making coffee. "It was a great conference, you should have gone."

"Did you get out of it what you wanted?"

"That and more, there were some great speakers, actually, turns out one of them was a friend of yours."

Morgan turned and smiled. "Oh yeah? Who?"

"Ryder Mason." Evan noticed the immediate change in her face. Although her smile remained, it was as if something came over the surface of her face to change it ever so slightly. "Interesting, I thought he had the same kind of shocked look when Ray mentioned your name."

Morgan recovered quickly on the surface. "I haven't heard the name in a long time, strange you'd run into him."

"He spoke at one of the meetings, a great speaker."

"He's a great pediatrician and a very charismatic man, it would suit him. Doesn't surprise me he was a speaker, just surprised it's such a small world." How odd was that? She thought to herself. Complete strangers that would cross paths and have her in common? Then again, there were many strange things that seemed to be happening lately.

"We were on the golf course, he happened to be playing in a foursome with us. Nancy called and mentioned you then Ray remembered Ryder said he was from Beach Lake. He thought there might be a chance you two would know each other since it's such a small town, so he mentioned it."

"Beach Lake is one of those everyone knows everyone towns."

"Is that all there is to it?"

"All there is now." Morgan answered honestly, she wasn't about to go into detail about her past.

"I hope it doesn't cause any harm, but Ray told him we were seeing each other, rambled on and on about the two of us. How he wanted you to leave the city and the four of us in practice together."

Morgan thought about it and supposed it wouldn't make a difference to Ryder what she was doing, or planned to do. Supposed he'd written her off and moved on, just as she told him to do. "What harm would it cause? Ryder and I..." She was going to say dated a few times but that was so far from the truth she couldn't make the words come out of her mouth. "It doesn't cause any harm, Ryder and I were over a long time ago."

Evan watched her move about the kitchen trying to busy herself making coffee, wiping the counter, and various other things. She began to talk of other things about the conference and he knew she was avoiding any more on the subject. Obviously it was something she didn't want to discuss, something she wanted to avoid.

He stayed for coffee but left before the girls got home so Morgan had a bit of quiet time she needed to settle her heart. Why was his name coming up now? Why had they run into each other? What were the chances? She thought of Ryder, couldn't get him off her mind as she wondered what he was doing now, who was in his life, who had replaced her.

She had no right to question anything of his life, she'd given that right up and couldn't think about it now. But she did think about it as she stood at the window in the den and watched for the girls to return. When she saw them, Morgan turned suddenly and knocked a wooden box from a table and it fell to the floor and came open. Then a little plastic ballerina inside began her circle dance even though she wasn't upright. Morgan bent slowly, mesmerized by it, it was where the girls found her a few moments later, still huddled over it.

"Morgan, we're home." Emily called to her from the doorway then saw her there, called to her again when she seemed not to hear. "Morgan?"

"Oh hey," She managed to say then picked up the box and closed it. "I knocked this over, I don't think it's broken."

"That's Amy's and she needs to put it up anyway."

Amy took it from her hands. "I've been looking for it, I couldn't find it."

"It's where you left it." Emily sighed.

"I didn't leave it there, it was lost."

"If it was lost, you wouldn't be holding it now. It wasn't lost."

Morgan needed their argument to bring her back to the present reality and she laughed. "Okay, we've established its Amy's and she can put it away now. Come on, pizza is getting cold, I expected you two earlier."

"I love it when you come, mom hates to order pizza."

"She makes us eat lots of half cooked vegetables." Amy complained.

"And things that are good and healthy for us," Emily complained also. "She's even growing a garden, her own spices and herbs too, it's getting out of control. Everything is organic, like she's going to save the world."

"She likes this life. She's waited for it a long time, let her enjoy it. You guys like it too." Morgan grabbed the paper plates from the cabinet.

"I like it here better than the city. I just wish she could still order pizza every now and then."

"You like it because Nick lives next door." Amy teased her older sister.

"Nick?" Morgan questioned.

"He's Emily's boyfriend."

"He is not." Emily disagreed with the statement but laughed. "He's cute, and Amy thinks just because I think he's cute that he's my boyfriend." Emily took two pieces of pizza and poured a very large glass of soda.

They ate pizza and had soda, another thing their mother didn't have often because Nancy had been on a kick of soy milk. But Morgan was there, and they stayed up late in the family room with movies and popcorn and junk food until they all fell asleep, all but Morgan whose thoughts wouldn't let her. The next day they went out to lunch and shopping, and the girls talked her into getting a much too short dress they picked out for her to try on.

"I don't know where I'll ever wear it to."

"Wear it tonight when Evan comes over, isn't he coming over and bringing Chinese food?"

"We're friends, I'll have to save it for a date."

"I thought you and Dr. Berry..." Emily began but Morgan stopped her.

"Your mother and father think Evan Berry and I are dating, but we're friends, and we like it that way."

"Oh, well then you should save it for someone else then, it isn't a friend dress." Emily laughed and shook her head. "Definitely not a friend dress."

Morgan laughed also, knew she'd never wear the dress at all but had purchased it anyway for their benefit.

"I'm glad you two aren't dating." Emily continued. "Not that I don't like Dr. Berry, he's very nice, but it's not what I picture for you."

"You're starting to sound like your mother, picturing my life a certain way."

"I don't think he's your type. You need someone more... I'm not sure, just someone different than him. I want you to move out closer too, but not with Evan Berry, I have a teacher at school that..."

"Please Emily, please, please, please..." Morgan couldn't help but laugh. "I will choke myself with this dress you made me buy if you say the words."

"I know you get mad, but I can't help it. I dream of growing up and getting married and all that stuff, isn't it what every girl dreams of? Being in love?"

"Told you Nick was her boyfriend," Amy smiled knowingly and Emily playfully swatted her.

"I didn't say anything about Nick, I'm speaking in general terms, and even you're going to fall in love one day."

"Ewwwww..." Amy scrunched her face at the thought of it.

"Don't you want to fall in love, Morgan? Isn't that what every little girl wants?"

Morgan looked to the young girl who was much wiser than her years. "I'm not a little girl anymore."

"You know what I mean." Then Emily asked her directly. "Have you ever been in love?"

Morgan smiled. "Love isn't as simple as it sounds."

"It is in all the fairytales we're told." Amy piped in then. "Like Cinderella. I don't know if it's love, but I'm going to meet Prince Charming one day, and he'll take me away on a white horse."

"I hope you do, Amy, and I'll be there to throw rose petals along the path for you." Morgan's voice was soft, if only it were so.

She enjoyed the day, enjoyed being in their life, one filled with little girl questions about love, all of them chatting and shopping and doing what girls did. But that particular weekend reminded her clearly that it was someone else's dream, yet another reminder of what had been taken from her.

That night after a ton of Chinese food was eaten, the girls put in the new movie Morgan had purchased that day and Evan and Morgan talked over coffee. He'd noticed she'd been quiet.

"The girls wear you out today? You're awfully quiet."

A weekend away to forget about things had only given her more to haunt her. "I'm sorry, I guess I am tired. We were up late last night and they had me running all day. I'm not looking forward to having to clean the house all day tomorrow before Nancy and Ray come home. We've made it a wreck."

"Different living with more than one person in the house, isn't it? Your place always looks immaculate because it has a bare minimum." Evan looked to her with kindness then. "When are you going to think about this life for yourself?"

Morgan sighed. "Not you too. Nancy, Ray, now even Emily and Amy."

"You enjoy it here. You enjoy being with the girls, maybe I'm starting to think like Nancy and Ray and want you to move out of the city, move closer."

"I like the city."

"You keep saying that and I can't find anything there for you. I can see a difference when you're there and here. Maybe it's something to think about."

"I don't have to think about it."

"What about Beach Lake? Ever thought of moving back there?"

Morgan shot him a look. "Why would you say that?"

"I thought the other day, just as I think now, that Ryder Mason means more than you said. Curious, that's all."

"Moving back there isn't an option, and it isn't something I'd want to do."

"What's your story, Morgan?"

"My story? I grew up and became a doctor."

"And you ended up in Minneapolis. Why? You had Ryder Mason in Beach Lake, how did you end up here? What's between you two?"

Morgan was quiet a moment then decided to share a little, just very little to pacify his curiosity. "We were engaged once."

"And?" Evan raised his eyebrows.

"That's it, that's my whole story. I fell in love with the boy next door, became engaged and it didn't work out."

He knew there was more she wasn't going to share and he respected her privacy.

They played all weekend as if parents didn't exist. Morgan let the girls give her that carefree feeling she got when she was with them. Life wasn't about responsibilities, it wasn't about appointments and women in labor and giving birth, it was about having fun, and she tried to act as she always did. But there were so many things that got in the way of her truly being able to push it all aside.

Much too soon, Nancy and Ray were due home and Morgan made sure the girls cleaned their rooms and helped her with the house so they didn't come home to a mess. She felt like the teenager who had a party when the parents were out of town, and she'd be scolded when they returned.

When she checked on Emily she found her room clean and found her sitting at the window and joined her.

"What are you doing?"

"Isn't he cute?" The young girl asked as she gazed out the window and secretly, from behind the thin curtain, pointed out the neighbor, a fourteen year old boy.

"Is that the famous Nick?" Morgan whispered back.

"Nicholas Edward Crawford. Even has a great name, huh?"

Morgan laughed only on the inside because she didn't want Emily to think she laughed at her. "Sounds very regal, and yes, he is cute. Why aren't you out there playing with him?"

"He was away this weekend, went to his grandmothers I think and just got home. But he doesn't even know I exist."

"I doubt that."

"Not that we don't do things together, but he looks at me like one of the boys. I think he likes Tracy from down the street. She's more the prim and proper type, always worried about her hair and stuff." Emily flipped her hair in a sarcastic gesture.

"I don't know, I think if he were interested in Tracy from down the street, he wouldn't be out there kicking that soccer ball around like he wanted you to see him."

"You think?"

Morgan laughed. "I think he's waiting on you."

They watched intently from the secrecy behind the thin curtain, could see him glance towards Emily's yard as if he waited for her to come out the back door. When he looked as if he were going to give up and go inside, Emily opened the curtain quickly.

"Hey, Nick, if you put the goal up I'll kick a few balls with you."

"Why do I have to put the goal up?" He argued.

"Because you're out there already."

"Well hurry up."

He said it as if he were impatient but as soon as Emily let the curtain fall, turned from the window and was halfway across the room, Morgan watched as he smiled and ran towards the garage. She was right, it's what he'd been waiting on.

"Hey, Morgan, think I ought to change my shirt?"

"Let the girl down the street be the prim and proper one, he likes you just the way you are."

Morgan stayed at the window a long time lost in thoughts again of her own childhood. The long ago day when she climbed the fence to Ryder's house or he to hers. Everything was before them, everything in the very palm of their hands, and everything lost to one fateful night.

In a silence that became a little eerie, from the distance somewhere, she heard the sound of the music again, the music of the ballerina. Was it real? Or was it in her mind? Morgan went in search of it and found Amy had left the box open in her room. The ballerina twirled with zest, almost at a frantic rate, but when Morgan picked it up the ballerina slowed, the music wound down then came to a stop leaving the room quiet again. She was holding it in her hand when Nancy found her there.

"There you are." When Morgan turned, for just a quick instant, Nancy almost thought she'd seen tears in her eyes but she smiled and the look was gone.

"Welcome home, have a nice time?"

"It was lovely." Nancy walked over next to her and questioned what was in her hands. "What's that?"

"Amy's music box, she must have left it open. I came in to turn it off."

"It doesn't play, that's been broken for ages."

"Broken? It's... it was just playing." Morgan knew she heard it, hadn't imagined it.

Nancy took it from her hands, closed the lid and wound it up again. When she opened it nothing came, there was no music and the ballerina didn't move. Morgan knew the thing was playing before, a few days ago she'd knocked it over and it played, Amy left the lid open and she'd just heard it a moment ago. She'd heard it play twice. The ballerina moving and dancing just like the one May used to have, the one they used to dance to as young girls. Was she losing her mind? She wasn't, she couldn't be, and she knew it had played. Strange, odd, and yet Nancy couldn't get it to work.

"I... must have a kink in it somewhere, I know it was playing."

"You might have thought so, the girls driving you crazy too, huh?" Nancy laughed.

Morgan was beginning to believe something was trying to drive her crazy but didn't say anything as they heard Emily's laughter from outside the window and looked out to see her and Nick kicking the ball around his yard.

"Has she been over there all weekend?" Nancy asked.

"No, he just got home, he was away." Morgan still thought about the music that wouldn't work.

"I wish there was a girl that lived next door, maybe she'd be interested in more girly things." Nancy sighed. "They're so opposite, Amy and her ballerina that doesn't work, and Emily and her ballgames."

It could have described Morgan and her twin sister. "You can't change who she is. And you can't stop her from growing up." Morgan would want to, would want to stop time right there and save her from the pain that would eventually come from growing up.

"I met a friend of yours, Ryder Mason. Nice guy."

Morgan stared out the window as if she hadn't heard the name, when again, just like when Evan mentioned it, it jolted her heart. What was going on? What was happening? Was she to be lost in some time warp forever? Was something unknown and mysterious trying to pull her back to the past?

Nancy watched her daughter and then watched Morgan with a little of that far away look in her eye she'd noticed when she first entered. She'd seen it before, and Morgan tried hard to hide it and push it away, but Nancy asked about it directly this time, something she'd never done before.

"What are you thinking about? You looked like you were somewhere else when I came in, and you look like you're there now. What's in your past, Morgan Bailey?"

"Something that needs to stay there, Nancy Wills."

CHAPTER FIVE

When the girls said that Evan had been over with Chinese food and stayed for a long time the evening before, both Nancy and Ray beamed.

"I told you he'd be great for you." Ray said, proud he'd set the two up.

"I hear you have me married off and in practice with you already." She mentioned the conversation with Ryder that Evan had revealed to her.

"I couldn't help it. You know how I am, I can't keep my mouth closed about anything." Ray looked apologetic. "I didn't do anything I shouldn't have, did I? That Ryder guy? He asked how you've been, I just filled him in a little."

At least he'd asked how she'd been, it was more than Morgan thought he would have, and she was surprised he'd even acknowledged he knew her at all. "That was fine, no damage. I just wish you'd tell me what's going on in my life before you tell others."

"He's a nice guy."

"I never said Evan wasn't nice, I like him tremendously." She didn't lie about it.

"I was talking about Ryder. He was still there when Nancy came and we spent a little more time with him."

Morgan watched their faces and knew Ryder would have been just as distant about her as she would be about him, knew he hadn't revealed anything. She smiled, didn't pay attention to the missed beat of her heart and the feeling of anxiety as she spoke with a casual tone.

"I take it he's doing well?"

"Has his own practice and was a great speaker, he certainly knows his stuff."

"I'm glad he's doing well."

"Strange running into someone like that out of the blue, who would have known?"

"Yeah," she said softly, "Who could imagine this world so small." She tried to hide the anxiety again, there were many strange things she couldn't figure out if she tried.

****

The plan she and Evan devised had worked and continued to work, only now, Ray was taking it to the extreme and had them married and living in the country with the four of them in practice together. Why did everything seem to be piling up on her? Thoughts of a life that wasn't, Ryder, the ballerina and the music, May's name from a patient. What did it all mean? Did it mean anything? She couldn't let it get to her, but it didn't help when there was a message from her mother when she returned home. Her voice had sounded a little worried and Morgan called her back right away.

"Hey, Mother, it's Morgan."

"I should think I'd know my daughter's voice by now, not that I hear it often, but I do still know it's you when you call."

Morgan resisted the urge to feel guilty or retaliate. "How are you?"

"I'm doing okay. I've been trying to get in touch with you."

"I was away for a few days. You should have called my cell phone. Is anything wrong?"

"I have something I need to discuss with you." Bea hesitated, wondered what her daughter's reaction would be.

"It sounds serious, are you feeling okay? You're not sick or anything, are you?"

"No, everything's fine health wise, I've never felt better. Of course my legs are a little weaker than they used to be and I have trouble staying on my feet for a long time, but that's expected at my age. It isn't about my health."

"Then what is it?" Morgan was anxious now.

"I'm selling the house."

The phone line went to dead silence. Neither said anything as it seemed time continued on without them and they were frozen there. What did she feel about the news? She'd blocked out so many emotions over time she was used to not feeling anything but numb, but this news was different, this news had an effect as emotions welled up in her throat, a sting of tears in her eyes. It represented an era of her life officially coming to end.

"Are you there, Morgan?" Bea asked, afraid she'd lost the connection.

"I'm here Mother. Why are you selling the house?"

"You don't know what it's like rattling around in this big old house by myself. All I hear are my footsteps, and even though it's not like I entertain enough to have to constantly clean, the dust alone takes me days. By the time I'm done it's time to dust again. I already have a buyer but I wanted to ask you before I did anything, maybe you're ready to move back and..."

"No," Morgan cut her off quickly, squelched all notion that would happen.

"You can have the house if you want it."

It represented a past she'd run from, one she escaped and wasn't ready to go back to now or ever, a childhood and a young adult life that was over. She didn't feel a need or a want to return to it, and certainly if she took the house, it would forever sit empty as she didn't foresee any future there.

"Sell the house if it's what you want, it's your house."

"It's your home too honey, even if you don't live in it. Maybe one day..."

"Sell the house," Morgan said strongly, there would be no 'one day', and there was nothing left for her there.

"Why don't you at least think about it? Give it some time."

"I don't want the house, I really don't. Where are you going to live?" It crossed her mind her mother would have a notion to move to Minneapolis with her and she cringed at the thought.

"I have a contract on a great condo in a retirement community. It's over near Hastings and they have all kinds of activities. Someone else takes care of all the grounds, and there's a restaurant, shopping, all right there. Even has a security gate."

Her mother's life was moving on and it almost angered her. "Sounds like you'll be happy there."

"We can sell the house later if you want. I can hold onto it and..."

"There's no need to hold onto it."

"Why don't you at least come home for awhile, maybe you'd change your mind."

Morgan didn't need to be there and knew her answer. "I won't."

"Then at least come out and see the new place, I can go to settlement anytime. I'll arrange it when you can come and you can take what you want out of the house. I'm leaving most of it, the buyer offered me more than the appraised value and wants it furnished, I can't use all that stuff anyway so I might as well leave it and start new."

Start new? How could she forget so soon? How could she leave that life behind her so easy? Her mother spoke as if she knew what Morgan was thinking.

"It's been long enough, Morgan." Bea's voice was soft, full of the compassion she felt for her suffering daughter.

"I know how long it's been, Mother, I remember it quite well." Morgan snapped. "Want me to tell you the exact days, hours and minutes?"

"You're still so angry and it isn't good for you."

"I'm a little angry that..." She was going to say because she was selling the house, that she could just move on with her life as if nothing had happened.

It was their home. She'd grown up there in the small town where her parents made their lives happy and content. As much as she still considered it her home, Morgan didn't want to go back there, she couldn't go back there, but she did always hold the notion that it would always be there if she ever could.

She had a wonderful condo in Minneapolis. Convenient to everything, three bedrooms, a great building with wonderful neighbors but she could still open a few closet doors and see boxes of things from her old life. Still not ready to settle in and call it a permanent home but she would have no choice now, her mother would be in her own fantastic condo and their home full of strangers, and it made it all so final.

Bea's voice pleaded with her. "I'd feel better if you came back first then made a decision. I'll get the new place and keep the house too if you want."

There was no hesitation. "I don't want it, I'm never moving back to Beach Lake, what would I do with it?"

"You might some day. Who knows?"

"It won't happen. It's just a house, sell it." Morgan insisted with the conviction she felt.

"Don't you want to at least come and take what you want out of it? What about some furniture, that apartment of yours is awfully barren, you could use…"

"I can't use anything. There's nothing there I need."

Bea tried to understand but was hurt that Morgan shut it out of her life completely. "Don't you want to come and at least see the house before I sell it?" She kept repeating it but Morgan put up a solid wall of refusal.

"You act like it's a feeling thing, Mother, I don't think the house will mind if I never walk through the doors again, its brick and mortar, wood and roof."

Bea was quiet on her end. It meant so much more, their life had been so much more, now she was alone in an empty house that Morgan would never come home to again and the sad reality of it made her cry. Bea wanted to help her daughter so badly but never knew how, there was nothing she could do to fight the demons that haunted Morgan to that day, nothing she could say to ease her pain.

Bea took a deep breath to speak. "Maybe you need to be back here to heal, I keep telling you that. When May died, you died too."

"May didn't just die, I killed her, remember?"

CHAPTER SIX

Out of a sense of guilt and obligation, Morgan promised her mother she'd at least come to see her new place, but told her she didn't want to stay at the house. She didn't even think she wanted to see it, so she would come the day she moved.

"I'll come the day you have to leave. I don't want to stay there, but I'll come to see your new place."

"That's great honey, can you at least stay a few days? Maybe a week?" Bea's voice was both happy she was coming and almost pleaded she would at least stay long enough they could enjoy it.

"It won't be a week, I know I can't get away for that long, and I can't make any exact promises but I'll see what I can do."

Morgan could have taken a week, she could have taken a month or two, any amount of time she wanted. Technically she could, emotionally she couldn't. She set in her mind she would go for a weekend and had a few weeks to fret about her return home.

She would feel horrible if she went, already felt the anxiousness begin to worry her, but it was her mother, and she would feel worse if she didn't go. Morgan knew it couldn't be easy on her to leave the home that held so much happiness for them all. Now it was only the two of them left. As nervous as she felt about going, the guilt of not going would almost be as equal.

The decision to go gnawed at her up until the time to leave. Her nightmares began again with full intensity and every thought centered on Beach Lake and all that was lost there, and on the eve of her departure the events that took place didn't help. It was a horrible night at the hospital when one of her patients gave birth to a stillborn child. Everything had been fine, but then everything had gone terribly wrong.

Morgan wanted to escape, to run away. Instead she took a deep breath and stepped into the hospital room with sorrow and sympathy for the woman there. It was the first experience for her and it rocked her to the core.

She took her patients hand and squeezed. "I'm so sorry, Beth."

The look in the woman's eyes was sadness, but there was acceptance there also. "I know it wasn't your fault, there was nothing you could do. It wasn't meant to be."

Morgan didn't expect her acceptance. Her child was gone, a baby girl who never got the chance to live, it was a devastating blow and yet Beth looked at Morgan with such kindness. Why didn't she blame her?

"Are you going to be okay? I can suggest someone you can talk to." Morgan began writing notes to be sure to give her the list of therapists and help groups that would be available.

"I'll be fine. What about you?" She could see the strained look in Morgan's eyes.

"I'll be honest with you, I've never had a stillborn birth."

"It's God's will." Beth said it so softly but it reverberated throughout the room.

Morgan looked at her in a daze, there was an eerie similarity to her voice, it was a voice she knew well, almost perfectly matched her own. The room became much smaller as the words still hung in the air, the walls closed in on her and everything seemed to go black, her vision actually impaired as darkness seem to fall.

"Are you okay, Dr. Bailey?" Beth saw a strange look in her eyes.

Morgan didn't notice the similarity again, her voice sounded like Beth's once more and not the voice of her dead twin sister. It shook her up badly on the inside but on the outside she held it together until she could get out of the room.

She was leaning against the wall just inside the door of the break room, still trying to catch her breath, when she heard someone else come in. Morgan didn't open her eyes until she heard the familiar voice speak to her.

"Long day?"

She opened her eyes to see Evan. "An understatement. Much too long and I think I've reached a point of no return." He smiled warmly and it was good to see him, a friendly face to bring her back down from the odd eerie experience, make her shake herself back.

"Maybe I can help. How about some coffee?"

"I need more than that right now. A drink?" She stated quickly her preference.

Evan looked at his watch, it was almost eleven o'clock at night. "You still haven't eaten yet, have you?"

"I have a half eaten roast beef sandwich on my desk, never got around to finishing it." She sighed, his timing was perfect.

"I think I can remedy that. The drink is your choice, but dinner is doctor's orders."

"I can finish the rest of the sandwich really quick, doesn't that count?" She started the process of leaving the hospital and he followed along and escorted her out as quickly as he could get her out.

Over dinner, he was pleased to see her color return. She'd looked so pale and stiff when he found her against the wall but she now seemed to look more herself. "You actually scared me. I thought for a minute I'd have to admit you to the hospital."

Morgan sipped the relaxing glass of scotch. She'd thought about wine, but knew she needed something much stronger. "My first stillborn birth, it took its toll on me."

"I'm sorry. As doctors, we place ourselves in blame's way, but ultimately, we don't hold the power of death, no matter how much we blame ourselves."

"Please don't say it's God's will." The words escaped her mouth. If he said it too, she really would think she was going insane.

"It is, but I won't say it if you don't want me to."

When he ordered several things from the menu the table became full of food, but Morgan barely touched a thing.

"All of this food could feed an entire small country." She sipped more of another drink.

"Morgan, you're working on your third scotch, that's more than I've seen you drink in the months I've known you. I know you're shaken up, but the scotch won't help nearly as much as the food. You probably haven't eaten in days."

She looked to him, his face genuine with concern, and it was nice to be worried about. "I've eaten."

"When? Other than the half eaten roast beef sandwich. And I'm beginning to believe that was probably left over from a week ago and not today." Evan laughed and began filling a plate up for her. "Make me happy, I'll only buy you another drink if you eat what I put on your plate."

"That's blackmail."

"It's necessary. If not, I'm afraid I'll be carrying you out of here over my shoulder."

"How gallant of you sir." She smiled at his notion to take care of her, then sipped her drink carefully, more slowly, to make it last in case he stuck to his word and she'd have to eat all the food he put there first.

Morgan seldom drank, but with each sip, it seemed to ease her fears just slightly. She knew it was no escape, she could drink an entire bottle but it wouldn't change that she would be returning to Beach Lake tomorrow after so long an absence. She wasn't looking forward to what awaited her there, so couldn't she get sloshed and forget about it for just one night?

She picked at the food and when Evan wasn't looking, she managed to slide a little back to its original plate and he hadn't noticed the difference. She couldn't eat, food wouldn't help, but the scotch tasted better and better. When her cell phone vibrated from her waist she almost panicked thinking it would be the hospital, but then she calmed, she wouldn't be available until she was back from Beach Lake, and when she looked at the number, it was Nancy.

"Hey, Nancy," she smiled apologetically to Evan who waited patiently.

"I left you a message at home, you're not there packing? Aren't you leaving tomorrow?"

"Yes I am. But actually, Evan stopped by the hospital and we decided on a late dinner."

"Evan?" Her friend said with a smile in her voice.

"Yes, Evan." Morgan laughed and Evan smiled.

"Tell him I said hello. I didn't mean to interrupt, I just wanted to tell you goodbye before you left for home."

The scotch was helping a little, but the reminder of her trip added a little edge back to her face. "Thanks, I won't be there long."

When she hung up the phone, Evan waited for her to say something but she didn't, so he questioned her change.

"Everything okay? Something wrong?"

"I'm going out of town tomorrow, just the thought of packing ahead of me still."

He knew it was more and said so. "I don't presume to know you well, but it looks like it won't be a little getaway vacation for rest and relaxation."

"I wish. Maybe I should just go to the airport and get a plane ticket to somewhere else, other than where I have to go." She looked at his kind face and decided to reveal her destination. "I have to go home for a few days. My mother is selling the house I grew up in, the house we've lived in forever, and I thought I'd be there for her."

"Obviously something you're not looking forward to."

"Truth be known, I'd rather spend another day like the one I had today, then go back there." She finished the last sip left in her glass and looked to him. "I fulfilled my end of the bargain. Do I get another drink now?"

He ordered it for her and ordered himself a glass of water, Evan had a feeling she would need a sober friend. "It won't help. It might help for tonight, but it won't help in the long run. What did you leave behind that you don't want to face?"

"You're very perceptive this evening." She said the words to avoid answering his question directly.

"Does it have anything to do with Ryder Mason?"

Morgan didn't let the name get to her, she let the scotch block it out as she laughed a little, said his name with a slight melancholy tone. "Ryder Mason. I guess you could say everything in my life has to do with Ryder Mason. But then again, he's no longer in my life, is he? So how could that be?"

The faraway look in her eyes worried him momentarily, he saw a vulnerable pain and then it was gone as she spoke again.

"I don't know why all of a sudden my past seems to be catching up to me at once."

"Want to talk about it?"

"And I also didn't know you'd changed your practice to psychology."

"I thought we were friends," he said.

"And I try not to burden my friends with things." Morgan smiled. "There's nothing to talk about, Evan, and it isn't because of Ryder I don't want to go home."

"Then what is it?"

"I left almost four years ago and there's nothing there for me. It's an empty, lonely town that…" She was going to add that it was a town that would probably be trying to run her out with lit torches just as they tried to do Frankenstein in a movie. The picture of it in her mind made her laugh. "It's just a silly little town that has nothing I need anymore."

"Is that what happened between you two? He wanted to stay there and you wanted somewhere else?"

"No, that isn't what happened." Morgan took another long drink. "What happened was that one night I woke up in the middle of the night and walked out the door. I didn't even pack a bag, just got up and left."

Evan looked at her for a long time. She was giving no more, saying no more, as he watched her close off again. "Hidden demons don't go away by themselves. You'll carry it with you, whatever it is, until you put it behind you. They won't just get up and leave one day."

"I know from experience that to be the truth. My hidden demons stalk me, they haunt me every day. If I get to a point where I can push it aside for just a little while, it isn't too long before they find me." Morgan looked across the room that was emptying of patrons, very few were left. "Do you think my demons are trying to pull me into hell? Doesn't the fact that I bring life into the world every day count for something, and I'll be forgiven my sins?"

Evan took her hand in his. "I can't believe you're even saying that. Dr. Morgan Bailey couldn't possibly have sins so evil."

"Killing people is a sin. It was the last time I checked."

"Morgan, it was a stillbirth. You had no control." He looked to her with that compassion that gave her the feeling he truly cared about her.

It was because of that, she didn't tell him the truth of her words. Didn't tell him she wasn't speaking of the dead baby girl she held in her arms that day. For if she told him the truth, maybe like the people who once loved her in Beach Lake, he would look at her with blame in his eyes. Morgan didn't want to see it, so she didn't correct him.

She wanted someone to care about her. Wanted someone to hold her and take away all the pain. It wasn't the act of sex she needed, it was the simple act of needing someone, needing Ryder, and if she closed her eyes tight enough, she could have pretended for a little while. So when Evan took her home that night and walked her inside, Morgan

turned to him and put her arms around his waist, pulled him tight to
her.

When she placed her lips to his, he slid his arms around her and
pressed to her, for a moment, taken in by her as he let his passion
overcome sense. When she began unbuttoning his shirt, and his hands
began to roam up hers to feel her soft skin, he pulled away quickly.

"No, Morgan, we can't do this."

"Yes we can." She tried to insist as her mouth moved to his neck and
placed soft kisses there.

"You can do this because you've had too much scotch, I can't do this
because I have a conscious and I won't take advantage of the situation."

"It isn't taking advantage, I need this right now."

"You need to go home and settle something."

She looked up and laughed. "Evan, we are home, we're standing in
my apartment, aren't we?"

He touched her face gently. "Morgan, go home to Beach Lake.
Whatever it is you're running from, go home and face it. Settle your
heart before it drives you crazy."

He should have given her the warning earlier, it was probably already
too late. She already felt she was going crazy with strange and odd
things happening all around her. "I can't settle it, Evan, I wish I could
but what's done is done and there isn't a damn thing I can do about it."

"If you think hard enough, I'm sure..."

Morgan gently placed her finger over his mouth and stopped him
from talking. "I'm a good doctor but I can't raise the dead. When I can
do that, I guess I'll settle things in my heart."

He looked at her a long time, knew she didn't speak of her first
stillborn birth, and also knew she was on the verge of closing him out
again. If he pushed, she would probably shut him out completely and
he wanted her to feel she could talk to him if she needed.

Evan looked to a beautiful face that hid so much pain behind brilliant
blue eyes. A smoky veil of mystery he would probably never break
through. He wanted to do something for her, only wished he knew what
to do but there was nothing, Morgan wouldn't allow it, maybe one day,
but for now he would have to be satisfied to at least know a little more
about the woman in his arms. A woman he wouldn't find it easy to
walk away from that evening.

But he'd promised her friendship, because of that, he pulled away
from her. "You're safe and sound, my job is done. Call me if you need
me."

"I need you now." She pulled him back to her as she whispered the
soft plea. "Stay with me tonight."

"You'll thank me tomorrow because I didn't."

"No I won't. I'll curse you tomorrow."

"Then curse me." He held her tight and kissed her cheek. "I told you, I won't take advantage."

"As I said earlier, how gallant of you sir," Morgan touched his kind face, wanted him to stay but could see he wasn't going to. "Are you sure I can't change your mind?"

"Not like this. I'd want nothing more than to take you into that bedroom and stay with you all night long. I probably wouldn't even make it to the bedroom. Maybe another time we'll have another chance but not like this, Morgan, I like you too much."

"And you love your wife."

He hadn't thought of his wife in a long time. It wasn't one of his reasons as he stood before this woman he cared deeply for and wanted desperately. But if it would help her understand his decision, he would somewhat agree. "And you, Morgan? Who do you love?"

She stood quiet and thought about his question. Why couldn't she love him? Why couldn't Evan be the one she truly wanted, the one she truly needed. He was handsome, intelligent, witty, and they had a great time together, she truly enjoyed his friendship. Maybe she honestly did just want to take it to another level, maybe the scotch and thoughts of Ryder had nothing to do with it. She was quiet as she asked herself the question. Why couldn't it be him?

He took both her hands in his and kissed her tenderly on the lips. "You love someone, Morgan, and I think we both know who it is. You don't have to tell me, but at least admit it to yourself."

Then he left before he wasn't able to pull himself away.

CHAPTER SEVEN

As she sat at the airport the next morning, waiting to board, Morgan dialed Evan's cell phone number.

"Good morning gallant sir." Morgan said when he picked up the phone.

"Well, I didn't expect to hear from you so soon." He had a smile in his voice. "How are you feeling?"

"Embarrassed."

"I was hoping you wouldn't say that. I was hoping you'd tell me you were awake and sober now and that you still wanted me."

"And what would you have done had I said that?"

He thought about his answer, there wouldn't be a question he would be in the first cab to her, wherever she was, and it wouldn't matter how far away. "I probably still would have been gallant and refused you. It's in my nature, maybe I was a prince in a former life."

"Then don't tell Amy that, she's waiting for her prince, and I promised to throw rose petals when she finds him." Morgan looked to the gate where the announcement was being made to board. "I just wanted to call and apologize, and also to thank you for not taking advantage of me, not that I would ever think you would."

"And risk losing my coffee partner? You're the only friend I have I can be sure if I show up at the city hospital in the middle of a snowy night, you'd be there. If I risked losing that, who would I have coffee with?"

"I'll only be the weekend. Maybe we can have some of that coffee when I get back."

Evan's voice was tender. "Call me if you need me."

"I'm sure I'll need that coffee date as soon as I get back."

"I'll have a fresh pot waiting."

As if there was urgency for her to settle it, Morgan felt like her past consumed her lately. So many reminders, odd and strange things, thoughts and nightmares to keep her mind in that other place in time and not let it go. She was so good at pushing it aside, tried to bury herself in work and create a new life and most times she was successful in hiding it away. Now, it seemed to be creeping out to her conscious from all directions.

May's name, talk of Ryder from a basic stranger who perchance happened to run into him, words spoken from a heartbroken mother who'd lost her child. Her mother selling her childhood home, one filled with so many of the memories she tried to run from. Why all of a sudden did it seem she was being pushed to face it?

Was she losing her mind? Her long hours making her hallucinate? Taking its toll on her already strained emotions? As the plane flew her closer to home, Morgan thought about the words she heard, it sounded so clear in her ears, her sister's voice as it filled the air, filled the room, filled her brain as she thought of it over and over again, the clarity consistent and steady.

It was as if her sister were trying to talk to her from the grave. It took a night of fitful sleep after Evan left to be convinced she'd been momentarily crazed to associate the voice with the words. It was impossible. She'd been thinking about her trip home after all the time that passed, and that's what made her think such notions. Morgan hadn't been back to Beach Lake since the accident. Guilt consumed her then as it did now at the mere thought of it, the same guilt that had driven her away.

People in town looked at her and cast blame, or so her paranoid notions thought. In actuality, they wanted to offer condolences but didn't know what to say to her, didn't know how to say it. Morgan saw their faces as shock and blame and it gnawed at her with unbelievable pain. Years previous, Morgan slipped away quietly in the dead of night when not even the dogs in the neighborhood were awake to bark disapproval. In her mind, no one would care, no one would notice.

Months later she finally contacted her mother first, then Ryder, who for once didn't argue with her because he was at his wits end. He agreed she should do what she felt best. He didn't know what that was anymore, and he never had, because nothing he tried worked, nothing he said had any effect. He obviously couldn't help her find the place she needed to get to and with pain and hurt he let her go.

"How long do you think you'll be? A month? A year? Can you give me some sort of clue?" He'd asked.

"Don't wait for me, I'm not coming home."

She said the words with a conviction that tore straight through him, a phone call, an entire lifetime together left to mere words between phone lines that stretched the distance easily and Ryder was more than angry and hurt. She'd made it clear and didn't have the decency to even face him. Wedding plans long since discarded, broken promises strewn in her wake, and a mere phone call to end it all.

Maybe he was wrong but he let her go. He couldn't take it anymore, it wasn't him she needed and he'd done all he could do, all he was left with was to hope that one day she would find what she needed and maybe ultimately she would find her way home. Morgan never contacted him again. There were no phone calls, no visits back to town, she literally disappeared into oblivion. Disappeared inward and every day fought the pain alone.

The plane landed on time but Morgan cut the timing close and made it to the car rental booth with just a few minutes to spare before they closed, she'd forgotten it wasn't a major national airport that would be open at all hours. Her mother told her that morning she would be at the house until six o'clock that evening and pleaded with Morgan to at least come for one last look. As she drove towards home, she thought of stopping and waiting until after six, waiting until her mother would have left, then gone on to her new home. But she drove on in a blind trance.

One quick last look was all she'd be able to bear and she wasn't even sure she could go through with that but she drove the rental car down the old familiar tree-lined street. The pang of heartbreak overwhelmed her. She'd never again have a reason to turn down Oak and make a right onto Birch, pass Rebecca Moorings house where Mr. Mooring looked up and waved from the porch before she made another right on what she always thought the most beautiful street, her street.

Maple Drive was where her dreams lay scattered about amidst the manicured lawns of the stately homes with blooming cherry trees that promised a beautiful journey to summer. Childhood hopes of marrying the boy next door and raising her own family right here, where time seemed to have stood still, flashed briefly across the front of her mind until she quickly pushed them away as stupid little girl fantasy's that life always turned out the way you thought it would.

She stopped herself from automatically honking the horn when she passed old Mr. Greerson's. He always used to sit in the window of the living room and watch everyone roll by because he couldn't take the heat of the porch in hazy summer or the chill of it in winter but he'd wave from the wide picture window. She glanced over but he wasn't there. Perhaps he passed away, she wouldn't have known and her mother wouldn't have mentioned it. Morgan told her long ago she didn't want to hear any neighborly news, so Bea never mentioned a thing.

When she pulled up to her house the familiarity of it was just as she remembered. There was not a bush out of place. Not a missing rocking chair on the large covered porch that saw so many days and nights of family gatherings, it now sat lonely, it had been a long time since laughter echoed out towards the front yard. The large white house with the black shutters held so much happiness at one time. It was all she'd ever known, the neighborhood she grew up, learned to ride a bike, kissed her first boy and became engaged to the same boy when he'd grown into a handsome man.

Her long ago dreams of buying a house in the same neighborhood and raising her own family had long since dissipated. The pain too great, she couldn't see herself living in the same place where so many dreams were lost and now that she sat in the drive, she wasn't even sure she could go inside.

She walked around the outside first. The backyard with its tire swing, the garden shed with old pots filled with dirt years old that never saw a seedling of any kind. Tools rusty as her father hadn't been there to pick them up and work the garden he so used to love. She looked over to where he'd plant tomatoes, cucumbers and whatever else he decided to grow but it now sat overgrown with weeds.

She thought about pieces of her life, but it wasn't just pieces, it was her entire life here. Morgan looked over to the largest oak tree in the town's history and saw the carvings of her and Ryder's initials. Her mind taken back easily to long ago times that seemed like yesterday yet seemed so distant at the same time. As if they weren't even her memories.

Morgan looked up to the back of the house and her eyes came to rest on May's old bedroom window. The way sunlight glinted, reflected off the pane, she almost thought she saw a face, the face of her sister. As she stared the face disappeared and just when she thought she could breathe, there it was again. The distance didn't disguise the sadness she saw clearly as if they stood a foot apart and both in the flesh. When the back screen door creaked then slammed shut, the vision disappeared.

"Morgan?" Bea said it softly, felt as if something strange was going on and she didn't want to disturb her.

The screen door noise of creaking and the slam of it against wood was a noise that was a constant in childhood summers of play. She could hear her father words... 'I'm going to fix that screen one day'... that day never came.

"Are you ready?" Morgan finally spoke and turned to her mother as she walked back towards her car.

She didn't want to be there, wasn't ready and would never be, there were too many ghosts to haunt her. The sadness of her sister's ghostly eyes told her that she too blamed her for death. I'm so sorry, May, she whispered inside herself. I'm so, so sorry.

"Don't you want to visit the house first?" Bea questioned.

"You visit people Mother, not houses. Do you have anything to take? I can put it in the car and..." Morgan couldn't finish speaking, she'd run out of breathe, began to sweat, felt hot and flushed and couldn't finish her sentence.

"I'll get my bag and close up."

When she was alone in the safety of the car she rested her head on the steering wheel and took deep inhales of air to regain control, she wasn't prepared for the flood of emotions that struck her. By the time her mother returned, she felt strong enough to drive out of the driveway and not look back.

They drove back through town and closer to the city where they drove around the secure neighborhood first. There were several pools, a very large community center, a golf course, and beautiful grounds surrounded immaculate town homes and condominium buildings. Bea was in a condominium, didn't want stairs, much preferred the easy comfort of elevators to be able to get to her sixth floor place.

"This is really nice." Morgan said when she saw where she would be living. Her mother would be happy there.

It was all her mother would need. Two large bedrooms, each with their own bath, a spacious living room and dining combined. There was a well laid out kitchen with the latest appliances and a large balcony that was partially covered and overlooked the golf course and a small lake. It was large enough for a table with four chairs and a few lounges.

"Maybe we'll go back to the house tomorrow." Bea said it casually, unsure if it would be an option.

"No. I don't need to be there."

"Morgan, you..."

"Don't Mother, let's not talk about this, okay?"

Nothing else was mentioned again. They had a small dinner of chicken and salad, a usual dinner for Bea as she was always consciously keeping an eye on what she ate.

"I hope this is enough for you." Bea wondered if she shouldn't have prepared something more substantial.

"It's more than I eat at home. I'm always grabbing a sandwich from a vending machine and might have time to eat half. This is fine."

"I've been trying to eat well."

"You're okay, aren't you?" Morgan questioned.

"Feeling better than I ever have, just want to stay that way. I've even signed up for yoga, I start my classes next week."

"That will be good for you."

"How are the babies coming along?" Bea questioned her about her work to alleviate the uncomfortable silence that fell between them.

"They're coming. Every day, every night, the world is more populated now than it ever was. I don't know why people are in such a hurry to bring so many babies into this world." She pushed the food along her plate, it was good and healthy but she ate little.

"Mildred Pierce just had a new set of grandchildren, Melanie gave birth to twins. Two little girls, I saw them the other day and I don't know how she's going to tell them apart, right now she puts a different colored outfit on." Bea hesitated then pushed it further. "Of course I told her it would get easier. You and May had to come into your personalities first in order for me to tell the difference. I had to leave your bracelets on for so long because I was always scared I'd get you confused. Somehow Henry could always tell though, he said..."

"I know what he said." Morgan cut her off indicating it wasn't a subject she wanted to talk about.

Bea continued anyway, "He always said you were the one with fire in your eyes. The same color eyes, the same shape, everything, but he could always pick you out no matter what."

Morgan rose and took her plate to the sink. "Everything was good, maybe I'll go take a walk now."

Bea spoke as if she hadn't said a word. "Maybe you ought to stop by and see Melanie and the babies, she'd love to see you, and you two were always such good friends. Why don't you surprise her?"

"I'm sure she's busy settling in."

"She'd never be too busy for you. You used to play with her all the time, I remember you two naming your dolls the same and May would always name hers something different."

"Yeah," Morgan put her plate in the dishwasher and washed her hands.

"You should have been the one to deliver them. You should have been her doctor."

"It would be kind of hard for her to make appoints in Minneapolis, the commute would be a little much." Morgan paid no attention to her mothers words, didn't want to remember what should have been.

"You would have been her doctor and Ryder her pediatrician, well, he actually is her pediatrician. Melanie takes them into the city to see him but..." She paused briefly with a second of hesitation. "And May, May would have sewn their clothes. She loved fashion, I think she would have been a successful designer, don't you?"

Morgan tried her best not to let her mother's words in, what point was it to talk about it? "I don't know what she would have been, no one knows."

"We can talk about her, it helps to talk about her and Henry."

"No it doesn't. I didn't come here for therapy, if anything, it makes it worse. I don't need to talk about May and Daddy."

"Maybe you do."

"If I do, I'll go to a therapist. Last I remember you weren't qualified for that." She regretted the angry words as soon as she'd said them. "I'm sorry, Mother, I'm a little stressed."

Bea spoke with a hesitant tone. "What happened to Mama?"

"What do you mean?"

"You used to call me Mama, I was just curious where that went."

Morgan shrugged her shoulders. In her hard cold exterior she even shut her mother out, she knew that, but there was nothing she could do to change it. She couldn't change anything, all she could do was try as best she could to live with it, and she wasn't doing a very good job of that.

CHAPTER EIGHT

"Dr. Morgan Bailey." Desiree whispered the words when she looked up to her then stood and gave her a welcome hug, held her a long time while she tried to hide the tears that formed. "It's good to see you, you look great. I wasn't sure you would come, but when my mother told me you were in town, I knew I had to try."

"I wasn't sure I'd come either, but it's good to see you." Morgan sat down at the table and ordered the same as her friend, a simple beer.

Desiree had her doubts Morgan would show up when she called with the invitation but was so glad she did. Her sister May had been her best friend and although she wasn't as close to Morgan, Morgan always interested in tomboyish things, they had been like sisters themselves.

"I feel honored by the way, no one I've talked to has seen you, and I feel it a privilege to be the only one. The whole town will be jealous."

"The whole town is probably glad I keep to myself."

Desiree looked to her sadly, it was obvious she still blamed herself for everything, still carried a burden. "That's not true, we've all missed you, and you left a hole in this place. You can't just pick up and disappear from a life and think it's that easy, think no one will notice you're gone."

"I think they'd all just as soon forget about me."

"No one ever has, and they won't. You're one of us." Desiree knew the words were true, but also knew she wouldn't be able to convince the sad girl before her of that. "How's your visit going? How's your mother?"

"She's great."

She couldn't help but notice Morgan looked so different from May now. Physical features were still identical but there was an edge to her. Morgan smiled, but there was hardness and emptiness.

"I couldn't believe she sold the house, but I understand it had to be tough for her trotting around that big old house alone."

Morgan knew she didn't mean the words the way she took them and teased about it. "You didn't say that to make me feel guilty, did you?"

"If I thought it would help you move back here I would have tracked you down and said it a long time ago, but no, I didn't mean to make you feel that way. Besides, I can't blame you for wanting your independence but I did hold out hope that maybe you'd keep the house for yourself."

"I can't even go into the house, let alone live in it." She admitted to her previous panic. "I freaked out just being in the yard. It doesn't belong to me anymore, it's a family house. It should be filled to the brim with something I could never fill it with."

"Is that who bought it? A family?"

"I don't know. The buyers attorney took care of everything, my mother didn't even know the name of the people who bought it."

Desiree groaned. "Sounds like city folk to me. They've been invading us. Started out they bought a few places on the lake here and there for weekend and vacation homes. Now they're coming in droves to live here full time."

"Drives the property values up, mother got a heck of a price."

"She's the first one to sell out to city people in Beach Lake. Our little piece of town has remained intact so far, but I know it won't stay that way for long. Only a matter of time." Desiree looked up when she heard someone call her name.

"Desiree, isn't it?" The woman questioned when she reached the table. "We met last weekend at your son's game and the barbeque afterwards."

It took her a few minutes to remember the name. "Stella. Yes, I remember. What are you doing way out here?"

"I brought a few friends out. I've been telling them about this place and they had to see it for themselves."

It was a casual place, a local establishment with picnic tables inside and outside, a great view of the lake and the best cold beer in town. Morgan looked at the woman who was maintained to perfection. Perfect skin, hair and a manicure she probably had a standing weekly appointment for. She had to wonder if she'd brought her friends because she liked the view, or simply brought them to laugh at the locals hangout compared to a trendy bar in the city.

Desiree didn't make introductions as the woman just said hello and quickly went to a table with the people she arrived with. Her friends were others like her, dressed in city finery and they were in contrast sitting next to a group of men just off a fishing boat.

"See? This is a local hangout and they're invading here too." Desiree said when she was gone.

"I take it she lives in the city." Morgan looked to her once again outside of the window.

"Actually she does," Desiree hesitated. "She lives with Ryder."

Morgan held any reaction she felt inside as she did everything else, she shrugged her shoulders and smiled. "She's pretty. Nice to know he still has good taste."

"I just met her last week when he brought her to the game. His nephew Jason plays on Steven's team and he comes to watch when he can. He's doing well."

"Great."

"Has a nice place, a new…"

"I don't remember asking about him." Morgan interrupted.

"I thought you'd want to know anyway. From what Stella tells me they've been living together and plan to be married before the end of the year but I haven't seen a ring and Ryder hasn't said anything."

"Well, I hope it works out for them." Morgan sipped her drink and took a handful of popcorn from the bowl on the table.

"And you're going to act like you don't care? It's got to make you feel something, you two planned on marriage practically since the day you were born."

"And we're much older now, things change."

"Yeah," Desiree sighed and looked pensively out towards the lake that was busy with those enjoying the day's sunshine. "Who would have thought?"

"Water under the bridge as they say." Morgan didn't want to talk about it but Desiree pressed.

"Not for you, you've built a dam and won't let the water through." Desiree took her hands in her own. "Your mother told me you still have a hard time dealing with it, Morgan, and I can see that for myself now. There was nothing you could have done and nothing you can do now to change it. It was God's will."

There it was again, the words, God's will, God's will, why all of a sudden did she keep hearing those words? First from a woman who'd just lost her child and now from Desiree, it was as if May called to her, as if she herself spoke them just like she had the night she died in her arms. Another chill ran up her spine when Desiree spoke again.

"I know she wants to help you, you have to let her."

"What are you talking about?"

"I'm talking about May," Desiree wouldn't let go of her hands, as much as Morgan wanted to pull away from her, pull away from the conversation. "She's the one that helped me through it. I spent a long time feeling sorry for myself, spent a long time being angry with God. And I know it sounds weird and strange, but one day at sunset I was sitting by the lake and I looked up to see this funny cloud. It seemed to spiral up to the sky and I know it was all in my mind, but it took a shape, I could see May there, as big as the sky itself, as if she hovered over me like a spirit."

Morgan stared at her without saying a word, she wanted to hear it, yet wanted to close herself off and she pushed aside the vision she saw in the window, it wasn't real, it couldn't have been real. "Funny she would appear to you and I've yet to see the slightest sign of her."

"You have to open your eyes and find her spirit, you've shut yourself off so much you can't even see her."

She didn't reveal she had seen her and her sad eyes cast blame. "I don't believe in that sort of thing. What's done is done and she's gone.

Why would she want to hang around on earth? I know I wouldn't if I had heaven waiting for me."

"She won't leave you until she knows you're okay."

"Well, she did leave." Morgan said the words to end the conversation and picked up the menu to signify she would talk of it no further. If Desiree insisted, she would simply leave.

But she didn't insist and they enjoyed an afternoon together. Occasionally she found herself glancing out of the window to the pretty woman Ryder had found to replace her. As far as she knew, there had been many in between her and Stella. The woman laughed with her friends, looked lovely as the sunlight glinted off her blond hair. It surprised her that his taste was so opposite what Morgan had been. A tomboy no more interested in a manicure than she was spending a day at the beauty salon to get her hair done. Maybe it all worked out for the best, maybe Stella was the type he would have dumped her for eventually.

"Why don't you call him?" Desiree asked when she saw where Morgan's attention kept wandering.

"Who?"

"Ryder. The love of your life."

"I guess if he was the true love of my life, we wouldn't be living in separate lives, would we?" Morgan played with the corner of her napkin. "I don't need to call Ryder, I'm sure he knows I'm in town, everyone else does. I suppose if he wanted to see me he would."

"And he's probably thinking the same way you are. You two are going to let pride stand in the way after all you've been through?"

"Been through? We didn't get through it Dee, remember?"

"But..."

Morgan sighed and rose to leave. "Not every fairytale ends with rose petals being spread along a golden path."

"Don't leave Morgan, I won't mention it again."

"It isn't that, I have to go anyway. My flight leaves in a few hours and I need to spend some more time with mother. She was playing bridge this afternoon, she should be back now." She pulled some money out but Desiree refused it.

"Don't even think about it. The next time you're in town, you can get the tab."

Morgan quietly laid her money on the table anyway. They both knew it would probably never happen, she would probably never be in town again, and there was a sad realization of that as it passed between them. When she left, Desiree looked after her, then when she could see her no longer she looked out to Stella who laughed easily, sat carefree and happy when it seemed Morgan's own soul had been shattered beyond repair.

When Morgan left, the conversation and all they talked about was all she could think about. The memory of that horrible moment in time that changed her life was prominent in her mind.

"Checking for malfunctions... charges may be filed after the investigation... nothing could be done to save them... personal belongings..."

The words of that fateful night rang over and over in her ears, drowning out the minister's words of solemn prayer as Morgan sat on the hard metal chair in front of the two caskets. The awning enveloped her in darkness and shadow as just out of reach was the glorious sunshine of a warm spring day. Her vision concentrated on a single rose among many making her peripheral vision nothing but a blur as she moved slowly into the trance like state she'd been prone to do after their deaths. Even afterward she couldn't clearly recall the faces or the names of the people who wished her and her mother well.

"Thank you for coming... thank you for coming... thank you for coming... thank you for coming..." Was the standard statement and it didn't seem to matter what they said to her.

She and May shared their mother's womb, shared their birth, shared their life, then why hadn't God taken them both to share death? Morgan felt like she had died yet still walked the earth. Why had he taken May and left her alone in a solitary hell she couldn't find her way out of?

As Morgan drove back to her mother's she was glad she would be leaving, it couldn't come soon enough. The town, the house, seeing Desiree, seeing Ryder's new life in Stella, it was as if the past and the future converged in that short period of time and she could see it all. Morgan knew this was probably her last visit for the rest of her life. Her mother could visit her, but Morgan wouldn't be coming back. The horror of it was too much to deal with.

Before she reached her mothers, Morgan called Evan from her cell phone.

"Dr. Berry." He stated in a rushed tone.

"I can call back." She was blunt and quick, she'd been in the same position herself to be interrupted at a bad time.

He of course recognized Morgan's voice. "No you won't, hang on one minute."

Morgan debated hanging up anyway but she waited as she heard several different voices in the background, then a door close and he was back to her.

"I'm sorry. I'm at the hospital, a friend's son hurt in a weekend football game so I'm doing a favor."

"I could have called back later, it wasn't important."

"Wasn't it? I told you to call me if you needed me, and I meant it."
He wondered if that's why she called, and felt better by telling himself
it was anyway.

"I just needed…" Morgan paused. She wasn't sure what she needed.
Wasn't sure what she wanted or why she'd called him. Then it dawned
on her, she wanted to see his compassionate face, a face that she didn't
see blame in, one that didn't cast a sad pathetic glance her way.

"Don't you get in this evening?" Evan asked when she didn't say
anything.

"My flight gets in at eight."

"If you're going to be at the hospital, I'll be in the doctor's lounge on
the sixth floor with a fresh pot of coffee." He didn't push her, wouldn't
meet at her house or make her feel as if she was obligated. If Morgan
wanted to see him, she knew where she would find him. If she didn't,
they would see each other sometime next week.

She packed her few things. There wasn't much but a small carryon
and when she was looking for her cell phone charger on the dresser she
came across a travel folder.

"What's this? Are you planning a trip to Alaska?" She questioned as
she took the folder with her when she left the room and found her
mother sitting on the balcony.

"I didn't plan it. I've been meaning to talk to you about it but with
the move and all I hadn't time. I didn't think you'd be interested
anyway."

"If you didn't plan it, then who did?"

"Your father," Bea said with a slight hesitation.

Morgan looked at the large brochure that featured a ship and
different pictures of Alaska. As a family, they often talked about going
but it never came to fruition. Her father's death was alongside May,
how could he possibly have planned it? Bea went on to explain.

"It came in the mail and then a travel agent called. He planned it as a
surprise for all of us for my sixtieth birthday. I assumed you wouldn't
want to go so I planned to cancel."

May's words reverberated in her mind, words that came from her
patient, words that came from Desiree's mouth… It's God's will… It's
God's will… why was she thinking of them again now? She stood
staring at the cover and a headline read… Find your spirit in Alaska.
Again Desiree's words called out to her. 'You have to open your eyes
and find her spirit.'

"Maybe we should go." Morgan whispered the words before she
could think about what she was saying.

"What?" It certainly wasn't what Bea expected her to say. "You want
to go?"

Morgan herself was surprised at the words that came out of her mouth, wasn't even sure where they'd come from as her brain didn't seem to be in sync with her voice, but the words came in a soft meek voice. "I think we should."

****

Morgan made arrangements at work to be gone and left the details of the cruise up to her mother. There were actually no details to work out, her father had planned everything from choosing the rooms to paying in full, all they had to do was show up.

They'd fly separately and meet in Seattle the day before the ship would depart and cruise along the inside passage to Juneau, Skagway, Ketchikan and Victoria, British Columbia. It would also cruise Glacier Bay and it sounded lovely, a dream of a lifetime, but all Morgan could think about was canceling. Tried to come up with every excuse she could but nothing sounded plausible, it all sounded weak and the lame excuse it would be if she did cancel.

The closer the time came, the more Morgan wanted to back out. Did she really have the time? What possessed her to suggest they go? Strange words that she put a different voice to, it was all in her mind she heard May, and yet it's what made her say yes to the trip.

Talk of spirits and heaven and funny clouds that she'd put credence into for a moment, now she wondered what had taken over her normally sane senses. She'd begun to think of odd things, put things together and then tried to shake the feeling. Morgan began to think different things were some kind of sign, the words, thinking she saw something in the window, all of it was imagination. Was her sister trying to tell her something? Talk to her in some way? Was there something she needed to do or follow? If so, what? Was it Alaska? Was it being with her mother? She didn't quite know what, but she packed her bags.

The eve of her departure had her restless and edgy. She tried to catch up on the news by reading the paper, then shifted gears and began cleaning out her kitchen cabinets, and it was all because of nervous anticipation to face what was before her, even when she didn't know what that was. It was almost ten o'clock that evening when her doorbell rang and she opened it to find Evan standing there with a lifejacket in his hands.

"I would have been here earlier, but I had some things come up and it takes a good hour to get to the city, if you lived closer, I would have been here sooner." He handed her the big orange vest. "A bon voyage gift."

Morgan had to laugh. "Something I certainly hope I won't need."

Her nervous mind that had been playing strange tricks on her immediately tried to interpret any meaning. A lifejacket. Was that a sign he could save her from drowning? Because she felt like she were. Stop it Morgan, she told herself. Not everything had meaning. Just because the sun came up behind clouds, or maybe it didn't, didn't mean anything. Just because you stepped on a crack or walked under a ladder didn't mean anything.

"And this," he handed her a small gift bag and she pulled out a cell phone.

"I have a cell phone, what's this for?"

"You know how service is sometimes with certain phones. This is an international cell phone, should get out from anywhere, anytime." He flipped it open and showed her his number already programmed into it. "Call me anytime you need me."

"You make yourself so convenient, you'd better be careful, Evan, I might start to get the notion to give your ex wife a run for her money." She smiled, touched at his thoughtfulness.

"She never could run very fast, you might be able to take her."

She made coffee and they talked until close to midnight as he helped put her kitchen cabinets back together. She'd not only taken apart one, but several, and now had things scattered everywhere.

"Did you start this little project just so it would keep you up all night?"

"I don't sleep much anyway."

He stopped and watched her vigilantly trying to force the lid onto a bowl but it was obviously too small. He watched for several minutes until she'd almost gone through close to ten tops before he sat down on the floor next to her, shoved them all back inside the cabinet and closed the door.

Then he turned her towards him. "What are you so nervous about?"

"I'm not nervous."

"You've tried every single top on that one little bowl. You pick some up that are obviously too big or too small and you try it anyway when you know it won't fit. What are you doing?"

She smiled and lowered her head. "You're right. The only solution is to throw them all out and start new."

"That solves the problem at hand, but it doesn't answer my question."

He was so close Morgan found herself touching his cheek, and in the next instant she leaned over and pressed her lips to his. Evan tried to pull away once, but she wouldn't let him, not this time. After a few moments they were laying on the floor amidst the different sizes of plastic bowls whose tops had been thrown into the cabinet, they entwined themselves and let whatever was to happen, have its way.

She'd unbuttoned his shirt and lay on his bare chest, kissed his neck then moved back to his mouth again as her hand moved to the top of his pants. Then all of a sudden it was Ryder's face she saw in her mind and quickly pulled away, sat up against the cabinet and apologized.

"I'm sorry, Evan," Morgan breathed deep as she leaned her head back and closed her eyes. "I shouldn't have done that."

Evan moaned playfully as he lay there with his arms spread wide and another aching need unfulfilled. "Not again."

"This isn't fair to you."

"I'm not worried about fair."

"I can't do this when I'm not thinking about you. I want you, I wanted you, but I'm not thinking about you."

"Even though I am but a proud, gallant sir, I have to say that right now I don't care if you're thinking about Godzilla. It doesn't matter, I don't care."

She laughed and looked at him as he still lay with his eyes closed in frustrated resignation. "But I care. And I'm the one with the conscious tonight that won't let me do that to you."

"Why does our conscious have to come at the most inopportune times? Always rearing up when we don't need them, it ought to be an option to turn on and turn off." He opened his eyes and looked at her hopefully. "Would it make you feel better if you called me any name you want? What if I said I'd think about someone else too?"

Morgan laughed again and took his hand in hers. "I really did want you."

"I know, until your conscious took over. I'm a doctor, I could probably figure out how to get rid of that condition." He groaned again and rose to sit next to her against the cabinet. "Want some scotch? A drink to toast your bon voyage?"

She entwined her fingers with his and held tight, then leaned her head against his shoulder. They sat there side by side for a long time in the silence until Evan spoke, his words spoken more to himself than to her.

"Ryder Mason is a very lucky man."

She didn't deny his words. Not even to reveal she didn't know if he was or not, she didn't know Stella. Not personally anyway, only that she was a strikingly beautiful woman who was on the verge of marrying the man she still loved, and there wasn't a thing she could do about it.

****

Morgan flew to Seattle and when she arrived at the hotel her mother made reservations at, she almost immediately turned and left when she saw Bea sitting in the lobby waiting with Ryder right next to her.

"There you are!" Bea hugged her in greeting. "How was your flight dear?"

"Without incident." She looked to Ryder and waited for someone to explain.

Bea stammered. "Ryder's coming with us, isn't that wonderful? Your father of course had a ticket for him and he decided to come after I hounded him some. I think I just wore him down and he couldn't argue with me anymore."

Morgan's heart seemed to have stopped, it took her a few seconds to speak. "I wasn't expecting him."

"Hello, Morgan," he smiled. There was no hug and not even a handshake one would give to a stranger, she made no move and neither did he.

"If I look shocked I am. Mother didn't even mention it to me." Morgan was furious and said as much to her mother when they were alone later after the small chit chat she could barely get through.

"Why didn't you tell me beforehand?" Morgan almost shouted at her.

"I didn't think you'd come." Bea made her excuses honestly.

"I wouldn't have."

"I didn't think it was fair to Ryder. Your father had this all pre-planned, he figured you two would be married and even so, you know Ryder was the son he never had, it was a gift to him as well so I saw no reason not to give it to him. There are three rooms, we'll each have our own separate space, and the ship is huge. I don't see where there will be a problem."

"You could have warned me." Morgan huffed and left the room, she needed to be alone.

With warning she knew her mother was right, she wouldn't have come, and Morgan wished now she hadn't let foolish words of haze influence her, but she also knew her mother was right that Ryder was as close to a son her father ever had. And even if they hadn't planned to marry, her father would have given him the gift regardless, would have wanted him to explore and enjoy the wilds of Alaska he often talked about visiting one day. It was something they'd all talked about many times.

"I'll be doing some fishing for salmon. What about you Morgan? You going with me?" Her father had said it with a small chuckle knowing full well Morgan didn't like to fish. "Maybe you'll be dog sledding or something else instead. That's probably more your style."

"I think we should all plan a trip to the islands," Morgan countered, "The beach, the sun, you could fish and I could dive."

"And there's probably not an island left that doesn't have a McDonald's on it. How commercialized is that?"

"It's convenient, people have to eat. What do they have in Alaska? A drive through that serves whale burgers?" Morgan snuggled closer into Ryder's arms. "What about you, Ryder, you're with me, right?"

"Can't say that I am, I'm with your dad in Alaska, as a matter of fact I'm thinking maybe we should go there for our honeymoon."

"Don't even put energy into that thought, it won't happen. I plan on wearing nothing but a bathing suit and I don't plan to be cold in it."

"Okay." Ryder said softly so Henry wouldn't overhear. "Never mind Alaska for the honeymoon, I'd rather see the bathing suit. But we'll get there one day, whether you like it or not. I'll drag you along and force you into snow shoes."

His last words were a little louder and May overheard. "Don't worry, Morgan, I'll make sure your snow shoes at least look good. We'll create some that make a fashion statement."

"No doubt you'll have a designer line of snow shoes developed and selling before we leave Alaska."

"That's not such a bad idea." May looked like she would seriously consider it. "Think about it, it would be a completely open market."

"Speaking of designing, when am I going to see my wedding dress?" Morgan asked. May had kept it a secret and she hadn't even asked her opinion or desires before she began making it and Morgan didn't have a clue what it would look like.

Ryder laughed. "You haven't even seen your dress?"

"Not a peek, she won't let me."

"So we'll both be surprised on our wedding day."

Morgan looked to her sister who smiled secretly. "You wouldn't do that to me, would you? I can't wait until the wedding day. I have to try it on, what if it doesn't fit?"

"Morgan, we're the exact same size and proportion in every way. And I'm your identical twin, I'll know exactly what you'll look like in it."

"May, you can't do that." Morgan was anxious and it was driving her crazy not to know anything about the dress she designed and created for her special day.

"I can do that, you gave me full control."

"But I want full control back now, I never thought you'd keep it so secret, even from the bride."

"It will be the most magnificent thing you ever laid eyes on, I've really outdone myself this time." May smiled with a satisfaction it was coming along so well and though it was difficult, she was so proud and anxious to share it, she insisted Morgan wouldn't see it until the day she got married and refused to budge. No matter how tempting it was to share her creation.

"You took advantage, I agreed to it the night we got engaged and I'd had too much champagne."

Ryder continued to chuckle. "You gave over total control, I heard you."

"I was delirious." Then Morgan sat up and looked towards her father. "Have you seen it Daddy? Can you give me a hint?"

Henry was quiet and lost in thought, he hadn't been paying attention to the conversation around him, had a far away look in his eyes.

May laughed. "I think he's still dreaming about Alaska."

"Or maybe he's dreaming about an island instead, actually thinking about it now. Sand, sunshine, warmth. Isn't Alaska cold? How am I to wear a grass skirt in the cold?"

"You can wear one around the house after we're married, I'll turn up the heat." Ryder whispered in her ear.

Her father was still far away in thought and Morgan spoke louder. "Hey, Daddy, you can come back from Alaska now and come back home."

Henry's attention finally came back to the present. "Always come back home, you can travel all over the world but you'll never find anymore than what's right here."

"I don't plan on going too far for too long." She snuggled into Ryder. "Everything I'll ever need is right here."

"Remember that, Morgan." Her father looked at her and Morgan thought she saw something odd in his gaze and then it was gone as he shifted his vision to May. "But I think we lost May now, she's daydreaming."

Morgan saw her attention wandering also. "Hey May, if you're thinking about the wedding dress again, it would be easier if you just showed it to me and asked for my opinion. What bride doesn't see her wedding dress until her wedding day?"

"But you're not just any bride." May answered as she lazily stretched her legs out in front of her and rested them on the rail. "Besides, I wasn't thinking about the dress, I was thinking about Alaska too. Unspoiled land, untouched by man, I can't wait."

Morgan laughed. "You sound like a brochure, and you're just saying that to butter Daddy up because you dented his car."

"What?" Henry asked quickly.

"It's only a small dent in the fender, and it wasn't my fault, Morgan and Ryder were goofing off and jumped on the car when I pulled in today and I couldn't see where I was going."

"Don't blame it on me because you can't drive." Morgan laughed and defended herself.

"Me? I can't drive? You're going to kill somebody one day the way you use that gas peddle."

Long ago words that had come back to haunt her time and time again, words she couldn't get away from. Morgan couldn't have known then, how true they would form.

CHAPTER NINE

The anger of Ryder there made her feel a mix of emotions. He reminded her of what once was, what she'd never find again. And unlike her mother and Ryder, she hadn't moved ahead, didn't know how. They easily left the past behind when it haunted her every solitary night, the horror of it plagued her and she couldn't let it go no matter how hard she tried.

Breakfast the morning of their departure was quiet. Bea and Ryder had continued to have a relationship over the years and talked frequently, more than Morgan would have imagined. But now with her in the mix between them, neither of them had much to say. She suspected her attitude had much to do with bringing the mood down but she made no adjustments to change it. What did she have to talk about? She didn't share their lives anymore, not Ryder's anyway and very little of her mothers.

The more time she had to think about it, the angrier she became. Was her mother trying to pull something, had she forced them together on purpose? Her excuse sounded reasonable, a gift from her father, but did she have ulterior motives? She also questioned why he agreed to come? Did his bride-to-be know he'd be spending the week with his ex bride-to-be? Morgan didn't think Stella the type to take it easily, so maybe he hadn't told her.

"I'm so excited, and I'm so glad you two are here." Bea commented with all the enthusiasm she felt.

"Don't plan on much for me, Mother, I have some sleep to catch up on." Morgan already began making her excuses as to why she wouldn't be spending much time with them.

"You have to come up for air sometime. There's going to be quite a bit to do on this ship and at the ports and we're not going to want to do the same things so I have a suggestion." Bea put down her coffee cup, presumed correctly that it would make their situation a little more comfortable. "We have breakfast and dinner together on the ship and everyone is free to do as they wish any other time."

"I have a feeling I'll find you in the spa," Ryder said.

"Getting as many massages and facials as this old body needs."

Morgan didn't say anything, didn't comment that she'd never known her mother to enjoy any sort of spa treatment. But she was glad her mother was going to have a good time and even happier she didn't expect her to be at her side the entire week. For whatever reasons Morgan had decided to come, now she pictured herself sleeping through it and getting it over with as soon as possible.

She should be able to get through two meals a day in Ryder's company. She was being pleasant now, smiled occasionally but added little to the conversations. When she finished her own coffee she left with the excuse she had to throw some last minute things together in the room and left.

"I'm sorry about Morgan." Bea said when she was gone.

"You don't have to apologize for her." Ryder too was angry, especially at the thought that she had someone else in her life, Evan Berry. And he didn't want to be there anymore than she wanted him there, which obviously wasn't something she wanted at all.

"Maybe this trip will help. I was going to cancel but she's the one who said we should come."

Ryder was surprised. "But of course she only thought it would be the two of you, she didn't know I was coming."

"That was my fault, but it's a gift to you as well, Henry loved you, you were a son to him and he wanted you to have this."

"You explained that, but I still feel bad that she's uncomfortable." Ryder looked to the elevator as she entered it, knew it would be an awkward week together.

"I don't think she's so uncomfortable, she still harbors such pain and I think she needs professional help, as a doctor you'd think she'd know that. She's such a different person and I don't even know who she is anymore. She couldn't even come into the house when she came to Beach Lake."

He'd heard from Bea of course, and others that had seen her, that she was there. He'd hoped and waited but Morgan never once attempted to contact him, it was yet another thing that angered him. "Maybe this trip will help. I would like to think it would help the two of you have a relationship again."

"And what about the two of you?" Bea asked with innocence, it had crossed her mind, but after seeing the two of them together she wasn't so sure now.

"Can't see that happening, all I can hope for is maybe a decent goodbye from her. That's all I think I'm looking for."

Bea didn't want to see it. "I think..."

"Don't, Bea, please, I'm not looking for anything other than that."

Why had he come? He questioned himself later. At first it was to see her and it was hard for him not to think their reunion after all this time would have been different, they'd been friends, had been since they could walk and talk and even with the shattered dreams of a much deeper bond between them he would have liked to think they would always be friends. He had to question that thought now, hard to believe they'd ever been friends at all because it was so strained between them. Barely a word was spoken, he received nothing but anger and hostility from someone he'd done nothing to, Ryder had done nothing but love her. Now his thoughts centered on what he told Bea, all he wanted from her was a decent goodbye, it was painfully obvious there was nothing else left between them.

Bea apologized to Morgan once more that morning before they left the room. "I'm sorry I didn't tell you about Ryder coming. Maybe I should have."

"Nothing we can do about it now, can we?" Morgan huffed. "I'll do breakfast and dinner but I hope you don't expect anything out of this mother, I hope you don't have anything else on your mind."

Bea had an unmistakable look of sadness. "My intention is to go and have a good time and I'd like to see you do the same. And I'm serious when I say I don't want you to feel obligated to hang around me. Besides, I don't think you could keep up anyway. I've become quite social since your father's been gone and I've been by myself, and I won't have you holding me back."

She said it jokingly, but Morgan didn't laugh. They took a cab to the pier and boarding was easy and carefree as their bags were checked and they went through the process. Her mother forced her to stand for a picture when Morgan would have bypassed that part of the process. The same rooms her father had arranged for had been kept, Morgan was to stay in the room that was originally meant for she and Ryder, Ryder would stay in the adjoining room meant for May, and Bea's room was a suite down the hall.

"Great," Morgan said under her breath sarcastically. "I need to be next to him for the next week. How wonderful will that be?"

Bea knocked on her door and told her quickly she was on her way to make her spa appointments and would catch up with her later. Morgan didn't know where her mother's newfound independence had come from. Was it new? She had no right to think she would have noticed because she seldom talked to her mother or saw her. There were many things about her she hadn't noticed before.

The stateroom was nice with cherry wood finishing. A comfortable bed, immaculately clean, and a large bathroom contained a separate toilet, shower and sink compartments divided by sliding doors. She had her toiletries with her and unpacked them, then looked in the drawers, turned the television on, and looked at the paper that offered all the information she needed on what was happening and where.

Morgan was restless and edgy. She wanted to call her office and make sure things were going okay. If not, what was she to do anyway? It was the first time she'd been on vacation for any length of time since beginning her new single life in Minneapolis. Previously she'd gone with Nancy for two-day jaunts but had never been gone from the office or her patients for a week. Now faced with it, she wondered when the relaxation would begin, if it would begin at all.

She decided on a tour of the ship and started in the beautiful atrium that spanned eight decks above. It was a fairly new ship and everything gleamed to perfection. With several restaurants to choose from, and an enormous amount of lounges or bars, Morgan couldn't imagine she'd ever go hungry or thirsty. Nor did she imagine she'd get to see all of them before the week were over, imagined it would take her two weeks to cover every inch of it.

She stopped by the reception area to get a map of the ship and a list of excursions to consider before she continued on through the variety of places, then went outdoors and walked along the promenade, watched the activity of loading luggage and other items of need for the passengers who would call this home for a week and there were many. From families, older couples, younger couples and a few single people, they all boarded with the excitement of a grand time, laughter and smiles on their faces. Morgan just hoped she could get through the week.

She dressed for dinner and met her mother in one of the lounges for a drink beforehand after finding a note on her door inviting her to do so.

"It's a beautiful ship, isn't it?" Bea smiled when she saw Morgan approaching.

"It's going to take me the week to find my way back to my room." Morgan smiled.

"Well that's a good sign, you smiling. I seldom see that anymore."

Morgan wasn't aware of how rare the occurrence was, so rare she guessed, her mother couldn't help but take notice. Bea stood with a few others who traveled with a group tour, all of them older and retired. She introduced them and Morgan sat down in an empty chair and watched her mother interact, she felt like she didn't know her mother at all, not the single Bea. She'd always been her mother and her father's wife, she'd never seen her as any other person but as she watched she saw how happy she was. Saw a new woman and not the same one she remembered.

Then again, nothing was as she remembered. That fact was brought clear again as Ryder joined them and he too talked with the group of people in his usual charismatic way. He'd always had the ability to meet friends anywhere and that hadn't changed.

Morgan stayed for a while and left with the promise of meeting them for dinner at seven that evening. With time, she continued her tour and stopped at a little corner on the main deck where a piano player entertained. It looked a perfect place to enjoy a quiet drink, or so she thought.

A loud boisterous man entered with a few other people and they carried on with a raucous, loud flair. He was older, Morgan would guess in his seventies, it was why she couldn't understand the clothes he wore that looked like he was dressed for Halloween. A sparkly blue jacket with rhinestones, a black string tie with horns at the collar to keep it together and a cowboy hat which he did take off when he sat down, but all she could say in her mind was 'trick or treat'.

She sat at the bar and he at the far end of the room. You'd think the space between would serve as a buffer, but she could hear everything as they talked of Alaska. Morgan could tell Halloween man had been there before, it wouldn't be the first time, and she imagined if she sat long enough she could hear all about his life but she chose not to.

Like breakfast, at least on Morgan's part, dinner was fairly quiet. Bea and Ryder talked about the ship and the destinations, Bea talked mostly of her new friends and how nice they were, they'd invited her to join them for dinner but she insisted she couldn't so they invited her to join them for a show later.

"You two are welcome to come along of course," Bea said. "Why don't you join us? Or I don't have to go with them, the three of us could go."

"I'll be turning in early this evening. I'll probably spend a few days sleeping to make up for my long hours last week."

"I may join you, but I'm afraid I may not last either. You seem to have more energy than I've ever had." Ryder replied as well.

"Both of you work so hard, by the end of the week you might be able to learn to relax again."

That evening was an indication of how the week would go. Of course Morgan didn't mind, she at first presumed there would be quite a bit more time spent with her mother but that wasn't to be the case. Bea had plans of her own and insisted neither Morgan nor Ryder feel like they had to be with her at all times, so the two were left to their own devices. They would stick to her mother's original agreement and meet for breakfast and dinner, and other times Bea flitted about like a social butterfly in a new colony.

After dinner Morgan decided to find another quiet place for a drink and ended up outside on the top deck, until the same Halloween man she'd seen earlier that day arrived. This time he wore what she could only presume was his dinner Halloween clothes. A black jacket with even more rhinestones than the one that afternoon and the pointiest boots she'd ever seen. He was with a group of people and they had to sit right next to her.

"Well hey little filly, what's a young girl like you doing sitting here all by your lonesome? And lookin' down and out to boot. Care to join us old folks? You ain't got to be sittin' there alone unless you want to."

"I was just leaving, but thank you."

He was only being nice, wasn't trying to pick her up and didn't say it to make advances. But her luck, he couldn't have been a nice young single man who would sweep her off her feet and make her forget her life. A very solitary one she was reminded of just by Ryder's presence. Instead he was an old obnoxious cowboy who probably lived in some big city and had never set foot on a ranch or a farm.

Before going to her room, Morgan took a few moments to stand in the quiet along the top deck. The air was chilly and the wind brisk, but she didn't seem to take notice as she was lost in thought, until Ryder stepped up beside her and spoke.

"I think this trip is a dream trip for your mother, she's become quite the socialite around Beach Lake, doesn't surprise me she's become one here as well."

It struck her he recognized a difference in her mother when she hadn't seen it before. "She used to be so set in her ways, didn't like change, and she seems so... I don't know, different. I never thought she'd sell the house and it didn't really seem to bother her when she did. Not as much as it bothered me."

"She asked if you wanted it."

"I didn't say I wanted it, it bothered me she could sell it so easy." She corrected his assumptions that she'd had second doubts.

"How long was she supposed to hang on to it? Isn't like anyone comes home anymore," he couldn't keep the insinuation from his voice. "It wasn't easy for her, she had a hard time coming to that decision."

"Doesn't seem that way. It's like she forgot everything, forgot what our other life used to be like and easily created another." It was more than she meant to say.

"It isn't that she's forgotten by any stretch, it's been a long time, Morgan, she's come to accept the fact Henry and May are gone. I see you're still struggling with it."

"How can you presume to know what I'm struggling with? You haven't seen me since I left Beach Lake." It angered her he could see right through her as he always had.

"I can see time hasn't changed you. You still have that same look in your eyes you did when you left. That same wounded animal look."

"I lost everything Ryder. Yes, maybe I am still grieving and maybe I always will but my entire world disappeared right before my eyes."

"That's the problem, Morgan, you haven't grieved yet, you won't let yourself. And you may have lost your father and sister, but everything else you didn't lose, you gave it away."

Ryder left before he said anything harmful in his tinge of anger that reared up and surprised him. Why did it anger him now? It was done, over, he'd said it all years ago, argued and fought for them until there wasn't an ounce of energy that remained. Even when he thought he couldn't argue anymore, he continued to try, to try and hold onto something he saw slipping away. Only to have his conviction defeated and trampled upon, there was nothing he'd been able to do.

That's what frustrated him the most, then and even now as he wanted to do nothing but hold and comfort her when he first lay eyes on her after all this time. His initial reaction wanted to take her in his arms and protect her from the demons that haunted her. But again, he couldn't comfort her then, and couldn't now.

Morgan was the only one who could find her way out of the suffering agony she lived and he refused to be drawn in again to a world she long ago made it clear he didn't fit into anymore. It still hurt and he only now realized probably always would, now that he knew with clarity it was never going to be the same again.

For the longest time, Ryder waited for her, prayed and waited for her to return. He tried to move on to someone else and couldn't bring himself to get involved. When Stella came into his life, she hadn't given up on him and took what he offered which was very little. Even now, knowing she had full commitment plans in mind, he couldn't commit to her in any way.

It was Morgan he thought about, Morgan he still loved. Then just a short time ago when he met her friends at the conference, Ray Wills explained Morgan's life in a way that pierced his heart. He'd met them accidentally and it was Ray that told him she and Evan were dating. He was proud he and his wife had been responsible for the setup and they were hoping to get Morgan settled down and into their practice in the suburbs. Ray felt since they knew each other, Ryder would automatically want to hear about her life, and he'd listened intently to words he didn't want to hear, words that tore his heart even more.

Ray couldn't have known that with each word, each description of a life he and Morgan were supposed to share together, it shot straight through like an arrow of fire. She'd found a life, just not one with him. They'd been connected since childhood, not only their hearts but also he truly believed their souls entwined as one. And there wasn't a thing he could do about it but live the rest of his life knowing it. It was the past, it was done and over, he figured out a long time ago he had to move on before pain took over his entire being, but he'd suffered through by waiting for her to come back. Now he would take the opportunity given to face her and finally get past it.

CHAPTER TEN

Emotions strangled her when she closed her eyes that evening. They forced her to finally give up any attempt at sleep and in the very early morning Morgan stepped out onto the balcony after pulling on a pair of jeans and her favorite sweatshirt, much needed warmth for the cold. It was bright pink with 'babydoc' embroidered on it in blue. The shirt was a gift from a patient that was well worn, almost to the point of fraying on the sleeves and had seen a better day but it was the warmest she owned.

It was instantly appreciated as she pulled her hands inside the sleeves and cuddled inside to protect herself from the wet chill, the mist that would become a standard. A weather prediction she would guess for the duration of the cruise.

Through the vapor of an early morning haze, she could decipher the outline of Alaska along the inside passage. Snow peaked mountains that rose in majestic glory, spilled its rocks and boulders where water and mountain met. She couldn't make it out, couldn't see it, but knew along the shore wildlife woke to a land that was still theirs.

Probably one of the few places left in the world that hadn't been completely taken over by man and the damaging effects of development, it was pure, simple, naked and bare in its magnificence. As the haze lifted, she could clearly see what there was to behold and its natural beauty humbled her, made her feel but a speck on its landscape, a speck that accounted for nothing, unimportant in the scale of Alaska's brilliance.

Morgan never went back to bed, instead she dressed for the day and met Bea and Ryder for breakfast in the dining room. Morgan noticed her mother didn't linger over coffee and realized she had plans to participate in a ship activity with others and left her and Ryder alone.

As the ship sailed through the inside passage, Morgan looked out of the window to be faced with Alaska's beauty again. How different the trip should have been, would have been had they taken it years ago when they talked about it. It wasn't meant to be like this, nothing was meant to be like this.

"I didn't particularly like your comment last night, about me giving everything away." Morgan broke the uncomfortable silence.

"I don't care whether you liked it or not," he said.

"Of all the pictures I had in my mind of us ever seeing each other again, I didn't think it would be like this."

"Nothing about my life is what I thought it would be like. If you think I'm angry at you because of it, I am. I'm not the one that changed it, you are."

"I couldn't stay there, Ryder. Can't you understand that?" Of all the people in the world she thought it would be Ryder to understand her the most. He was there when they got to the hospital that night and she'd begged and pleaded with him to save her sister and her father who were already dead. He saw first hand the wrenching pain that took hold and never let go, and because of that she'd always expected understanding.

"And you think you're the only one who's suffered through all this?"

"I don't think that, but I think I've suffered more. I was there, I killed them."

"The only person you're guilty of killing is yourself, Morgan. You suffered two deaths but I suffered three because I had to watch you die too. Night after night I watched you die until you ran away from it all, and the hardest part for me is I couldn't do a damn thing to help you. You wouldn't let me help, but..." He was about to say she'd found someone else to console her, but stopped himself.

"I wouldn't what? What were you going to say, Ryder, I wouldn't forget about it? I wouldn't let it go like you and mother have done? Well somebody has to remember them if you two don't." Her words were harsh.

Ryder put his cup down and rose to leave. "Be angry if you have to, whatever helps, but don't be angry with me. I've never done anything but love you."

He didn't run into her the rest of the day, heard her a few times when he was on his balcony and her balcony door opened or closed. Ryder sat in silence knowing she was probably just on the other side of the partition. Odd they once shared so much and now couldn't even exchange friendly words.

They'd shared peanut butter and jelly sandwiches on a creaky porch swing when they were six, to their bed just a few short years ago, those few years felt like an eternity ago now. As he closed his eyes and felt the mist on his face, he thought of the person she used to be. Vibrant, exciting, there was nothing Morgan feared in life, lived it to the fullest. One thing that haunted him most was her laughter, a sound that rang free and content, he missed it now, along with everything else she'd once been.

On the other side of the barrier, Morgan had to keep her thoughts from swaying towards Ryder, and thought about her mother. She was out and about the ship that day, but Morgan didn't run into her at all and began to think about not spending time with her. Had she moved so far away from her that there was no getting back to where they once were?

"Don't feel like you have to coddle me and hang around me, we're both here to have fun." Her mother told her the moment they'd arrived at the ship.

Morgan was happy to see she'd found some independence, but in a way it made her begin to feel lonely, even lonelier than she normally did, as if her mother didn't need her. But that was a stupid thought and she knew it. Morgan hadn't been there for her, had left her alone to fend for herself and had no right to complain now. Ryder had been right and she knew that too, she didn't lose her mother, she'd let her go.

Most of her day was doing as she said the evening before, without her cell phone or beeper going off, with no interruptions, she slept. Morgan napped in bed, on the balcony, and in a lounge chair on the top deck when she sat to read a book she purchased. It was always easier for her to sleep in the light of day, it was when the dark of night came she had trouble, so she napped on and off that day and by the time she was getting ready for dinner she felt rested and a little more relaxed.

Morgan looked into the mirror while she put her makeup on. It was never her face that looked back, she hadn't seen her true self since May's death, and it was May she saw now as she always did. Morgan knew the little differences no one else could ever see. Maybe she saw May's face all the time as a way of keeping her with her, a way of keeping her alive.

"There you are, don't you look great this evening." Bea smiled at Morgan who did look lovely in a simple black turtleneck dress. Her dark hair pulled back and dangly earrings hung from her ears.

"I had to dress, I've been running around in sweats all day and if I didn't get out of them I was afraid I'd go back to bed."

"Back to bed? There's so much to do on this ship, so much to see." Bea exclaimed as if it were a crime to sleep.

"I saw it from my balcony between naps."

Bea had been waiting outside of the dining room door and Morgan mistakenly thought she'd been waiting for her. When she spoke, she realized it wasn't her she waited for.

"I've invited a friend for dinner, I hope you don't mind that I did."

"Of course not." Morgan shrugged her shoulders.

"Ryder's already at the table, I'll be inside in just a few minutes."

She joined Ryder and ordered a drink while they waited.

"Did you have a good day?" Ryder asked.

"I did," she answered then added as an afterthought. "You?"

"Are you asking because you're interested?"

Morgan looked up at him, hesitated at first then answered honestly. "No, just asked for menial conversation purposes."

"That's what I thought." Ryder chuckled and continued to glance over the menu. Then he said what he'd been thinking. "You did this when we were kids."

"Did what?" She looked at him suspiciously, didn't know what he spoke of.

"You fought me every step of the way, maybe that's what you're doing now."

"We're not doing anything now but disagreeing. You can easily forget about death and I can't."

"Is that why we're disagreeing?" Ryder looked up from his menu and wanted an honest answer.

"We obviously don't mean anything to each other anymore, what else would we have to disagree on?"

"So there it is. We don't mean anything to each other anymore." He repeated her statement with a strange even tone to his voice. "And you came to that decision by yourself without even considering my opinion?" He leaned closer to her, gave her his full attention and waited. He wasn't going to walk on the eggshells around her, he'd decided to barrel right through.

"Are you saying we mean something to each other? Seems I have to disagree on that also." Morgan huffed in defiance.

In the quiet between them, she thought of Stella and he thought of Evan. Thoughts of a person they'd once dedicated their life to, committed to other people now, whether true or not, sat between them unknown in the middle of the table as if it were a centerpiece.

Ryder was the first to speak. "We settled our differences back then, I could suggest we do it the same way now, but you probably won't like it."

Ryder didn't say anything else, he picked the menu up again and left her sitting there silently questioning what he spoke of. Finally, her curiosity got the best of her and she had to ask.

"How did we settle it then? What do you suggest?"

"You fought me every step of the way when we were kids, but the first time we made out it was all over. Maybe we should go somewhere and make out and get it over with."

Morgan would have slammed him with words but she looked up to see her mother approaching and her problems escalated quickly. Bea was accompanied by the overgrown cowboy she'd seen several times on the ship with the same type of festival clothing she'd seen him in. This time he wore a bright red jacket with silver trim, loud obnoxious belt buckle, and snakeskin cowboy boots with long pointy tips that looked sharp enough to make meticulous cuts to perform surgery. Along with his gaudy dress, she immediately recognized something about her mother. Bea looked different, oh my God, she was glowing, Morgan screamed silently in her brain. Smiling and glowing like an infatuated schoolgirl with a huge crush on this larger than life garish cowboy. Immediately, her protection instincts went into gear.

Bea didn't have to make introductions, Jerry immediately greeted them as if he'd been in their lives all along. "Morgan, so nice to finally be able to sit down and break bread, I been seeing you all over the ship but you won't talk to me, now you won't be able to get away." Then he turned to Ryder. "Good to see you again, Ryder. We got to talk, I been listening to stories about you all day, dang near close to God in Bea's opinion."

"An opinion I'm afraid that's certainly inflated." Ryder had to laugh.

Jerry spoke and said things as if he knew her and it irritated Morgan. Who was this strange man who would presume to know her? Take minimal information her mother supplied and turn it into something that made them less than strangers. She didn't say much of anything and thankfully he moved on to other subjects. Ryder was more accommodating, he chatted with him, even laughed at his corny jokes.

"Bea tells me all about you two growing up as little one's, nice to have lifelong friends, nothing like them."

"I'm surprised you'd have any friends to know the difference." Her harsh words escaped and Morgan stood to leave.

"Morgan," Bea said the words loudly as if she were going to scold her.

"I don't like the fact that this stranger thinks he knows all about us. My life is not his business and I won't make it his business, I'd appreciate it if you did the same and kept me out of your conversations." Morgan couldn't sit any longer in his company, couldn't talk about things she didn't wish to talk about with a stranger. A garish, overgrown cowboy who knew nothing of her life and she planned to keep it that way.

"Where you going, little filly, out to lasso yourself up some fun?"

"I wish you'd stop calling me that, I'm not a horse." Morgan stared at him then left as she heard his laughter behind her.

Ryder also excused himself and left the two alone over their coffee and all the desserts Jerry ordered for them to share a little of each.

"Whew, that gal has one helluva' big ole' chip on her shoulder. Don't suppose she takes kindly to me, or is that the way she is with all new friends?"

"I told you she'd be tough. She didn't used to be that way but she shuts herself off so much now." Bea answered as she watched her daughter leave the room and Ryder behind her. "She's never gotten over her father and sisters death. No one expects it to be easy, and I still carry my own baggage, but Morgan, I'm afraid there's been nothing to help her through this."

"She has more than baggage she's carrying around, she's cartin' the whole dang luggage set. Garment bag, carry on, massive baggage and she ain't even using the wheels, she's lugging it all on her shoulders. It's been awhile, hasn't it? I don't mean to sound callous, but I would think she'd have found a better place by now."

Bea was quiet for a moment then offered him further explanation. "It's been a little more difficult and complicated for her. Morgan was driving the car when they were killed."

****

Morgan found a quiet spot on the deck to get away from everything and second guessed, once again, her decision to come. What did she think she'd find here? Maybe she could take a plane out of Juneau tomorrow. Leave her mother and Ryder and go back to Minneapolis, go back to her office and her patients. They probably wouldn't notice she was even gone, they seemed to be able to function quite well without her.

"Don't you think you were a little rough on Jerry?" Ryder asked as he walked up behind Morgan who stood at the banister looking out to sea.

Morgan used a phrase she found Jerry was fond of. "If that 'sum'bitch' thinks I'm going to stand by and watch him take advantage of my mother, his cowboy hat is way too tight."

"Your mother's a grown woman, I think she knows what she likes and doesn't by now. She's lonely, Morgan. There's nothing wrong with a little companionship, and if she finds it in someone like Jerry, why not?"

She thought of Ryder doing the same thing, only his had been Stella and probably tons of others in between that came before his wife to be. "Well, I don't like him."

"He might dress a little loud and say things a little different than the rest of us, but I have to say, I like him. Maybe if we all said everything that came to our minds things would be simpler."

"How can you say that? You don't think he's totally taking advantage of her? A lonely woman who's comfortable financially, and most vulnerable, she makes herself a perfect target for someone like Jerry."

He liked the fact Morgan worried about her mother, it was more than she had in the last few years and if it took someone like Jerry to make her take notice, he wasn't going to spoil it by revealing she had no worries that Jerry was looking at her pocketbook. He met Jerry the previous evening and also spent some time with him and Bea that day.

Bea seemed to be taken by him and although Ryder liked him, like Morgan, he had his own secret reservations out of protection for Bea. He imagined there were people who preyed on widows and as he was passing some time on the Internet decided to check him out a little and found out some things about Jerry but didn't reveal it. Ryder stayed with his first instinct and let Morgan worry about her mother, it had been far too long since she had.

"She doesn't even act like herself anymore, she's a person I hardly know." Morgan spoke the words out loud when she hadn't meant to.

"I have to admit she's changed, but that isn't a bad thing. She doesn't have anyone to pamper, or nurture and you've gone on with your own life and don't need her anymore."

"And you have to point that out to make me feel guilty?"

"I just made a statement and if you feel guilty that's your own doing." Ryder continued before she could stop him again. "She's come to terms with being a widowed single woman."

"Does she date at home?" Morgan asked. It was something she hadn't asked her mother directly, nor ever considered.

"I keep an eye on her and make sure she's doing okay. I've always stopped in to see if she needs anything, fix a few things around the house when I can. I don't ask about her personal life, it's none of my business. But I do think she's gone out a few times."

Morgan looked out to the moonlight as it trickled across the water and headed straight for her. The air was chilly and brisk, the stars phenomenal as they gathered in mass in the dark of night. In a way, she envied her mother, even if she worried about her judgment.

When she spoke her voice was soft, offered the only thing she could think why she couldn't do the same as Bea had, it hadn't been so easy for her. "It's like my right arm is missing. You know if you hurt your hand or something and have to use your left how awkward it is? It's like that for me all the time. That's how I've felt since... since the accident. I'd depended on something and now it's gone, and for the rest of my life there will be something missing."

"Maybe you came here to find what was missing." Ryder commented as he leaned comfortably against the banister. "Think about it, why did you come?"

"I don't know, I keep asking myself that same question. There were some things..." She stopped, didn't want to sound foolish.

"There were some things?" He raised his eyebrows.

"Call them signs. Call them hallucinations due to lack of sleep that I took as signs."

Ryder decided to push it since she seemed to be in the mood to talk. "Like?"

"I met with Desiree when I was at Beach Lake and she said something about May's spirit, then I saw the cruise brochure and it touted 'Find your spirit in Alaska'. And... well, maybe a few other things but it's all ridiculous."

"You don't think the signs are real? You don't think the timing of your mother selling the house and getting the tickets in the mail is more than coincidence? Desiree's words and you seeing them right after? Did you not come looking for it? Even in your subconscious mind, even if you don't think it real, you have to admit you're here in Alaska for something. A month ago did you think you'd be here?"

"Of course not, but that doesn't mean anything."

"Doesn't it?" Even in the dark of night, just the moonlight that glinted in her eyes he could see the sadness. "Even they're trying to help you, Morgan, I hope you let them."

Ryder then walked away.

****

'God's will'... 'God's will'... the words rang over and over in her mind as Morgan tried to get to sleep that evening, it was the main sign that drove her to the beauty of Alaska for still mysterious reasons. As she finally made it into sleep it wouldn't be restful, she relived that horrible night in every vivid detail.

Life was just on the verge of happening when it all came crashing down. She and Ryder had come through their childhood as one and were about to be married. He was about to start his career as a pediatrician and she as a gynecologist. Funny, she delivered life now. Delivered life almost every day of the week, yet it was ironic she had none of her own.

And each time she held a brand new baby in her arms she looked for May or her father as if they'd be reborn somehow and Morgan would see it. Maybe in her subconscious mind with each life she brought into the world it would erase the two deaths she caused.

Seeing Ryder brought back so much of what happened. Long ago she learned how to push it deeply inside where the details of it were all fuzzy, but seeing him made everything surface so clearly and as she lay in bed that evening she relived the entire night.

They'd met Ryder for dinner in the city that night when Bea was home sick with a cold. Her mother rested and she didn't want to eat, so Morgan and May talked their father into going out with them. Ryder had to work a late shift at the hospital so they'd surprised him.

It had been a wonderfully relaxing evening and when Ryder had to go back to work, their jovial attitudes continued on the way home. Morgan drove and May was in the passenger seat, they laughed at their father in the back seat pretending to keep up with the words to a popular song she and May were following along to on the radio.

"Isn't this your favorite song Daddy?" May teased.

"I have it on eight track at home," he joked back.

"Don't tell anyone that, it's a CD nowadays. A little silver disk, remember?"

"Wasn't anything wrong with the eight track."

Morgan heard the loud noise of a truck brake and horns but didn't have time to react as the tractor-trailer bore through the intersection at full speed. Her mind tried to react but she didn't understand, her light was green, it shouldn't be happening, but it happened just as she was in the middle of the road and couldn't do a thing. She heard the noise and looked to see the glare of headlights just before the tremendous impact. There were several other cars behind her that were also involved in the wreckage but nowhere near the extent they were as her car was hit square on the passenger side where both May and her father sat.

Morgan didn't remember how far they'd traveled on the trucks front bumper until the truck turned over then they went airborne, rolled, tossed and turned many times before they came to a slamming halt. Nor did she remember how many seconds, minutes or hours passed before they finally came to a stop. Clearly in her mind were the screams, the terror, the noise of people shouting and crying, the fear in their voices, then the sound of sirens and police radios, it all jumbled together but she remembered it well in her nightmares, all in slow motion detail.

When the car finally did come to a rest, Morgan was the only one left inside, the entire side of the car her father and May had been on was ripped off completely, the car torn in half. She'd passed out for a few brief seconds but in her mind she knew she had to get out, had to get out to help, but when she came to she couldn't get out. Her side of the car was wedged against a huge tree so she managed with great pain to climb over the passenger seat where May once sat. Now there was nothing but blood and mangled metal that had replaced her, and then through a haze she saw her sister laying on the ground, her father only a few feet away. Somehow, Morgan's mind knew instantly her father was dead. She tried to walk, to run, but stumbled, then crawled to May who lay bleeding and torn on black asphalt pavement.

"What the heck took you so long?" May sputtered the words out, with every word, blood rolled down her chin.

"I'm so sorry, I'm so sorry I didn't see it, I don't even know what hit us."

"Shhhhhh... No, Morgan, it isn't your fault." May's face twisted in pain.

"You'll be all right. Stay with me and just keep talking, you're going to be all right. Help is on the way."

"No help... I've... I've been waiting to say goodbye." Her voice was a blood filled gurgle.

"No, May, don't talk like that, you're not going anywhere."

"I have to. It's God's will."

Morgan pleaded with her dying sister. "Stay with me, please, just stay here with me. We're not saying goodbye, it isn't time."

"It is time, I don't know why, but I'm not afraid." She coughed and blood spurt all over Morgan's face and mixed with her own from the long gash in her head. "Don't worry about me, I'm not afraid."

"Talk to me, May, yesterday you were talking about the songs we should have at the wedding reception. You told me your favorites you wanted to dance to, tell me May, talk to me." Morgan used her bare hand and wiped away the blood that rolled down her chin and onto her neck.

"You'll dance, Morgan, you'll dance."

Morgan picked her sister's battered head up gently and felt an open hole in the back of her skull, could feel the bone on her tender palm as warm blood covered it immediately. So much blood, she felt it in her hand, sat in a puddle of it around her on the hard ground, and even though May's face appeared not to have been damaged at all, blood continued to trickle out of her mouth.

"You'll dance too May, we're both going to dance, you can't go anywhere, hang on."

"Like the ballerina..." May sputtered more, "Like the ballerina in the music box."

Morgan began to cry harder and choked on her tears, she could feel her sister going as if she were inside her battered body, as if she felt every pain and dying emotion, as if their heart truly did beat as one. "I remember, we danced to it all the time. Remember, May? Remember we used to dress up and dance with the ballerina. You made me wear that tutu." Morgan laughed nervously, her voice a desperate plea now. "I remember, May, let's talk about it. Don't leave me, please don't leave me."

"I have to but you'll be okay, you'll dance with the ballerina again, you'll dance."

"You will too, May, we both will. I'll put on whatever you want me to wear and we'll do it just like when we were kids. Just stay with me, you have to stay awake."

May talked slowly as life eased out of her and spewed across the ground around them. "My twin, my immortality, how lucky we are to have two of us, huh Morgan? You stay with Mama and I'll go with Daddy."

As she held her sisters head gently, her other hand over May's heart, Morgan felt the exact moment when life passed. Her own heart stopped beating as if she too suffered death the instant May did. Her tears landed on her sister's face as if they could wash away the blood and her cry and shrill plea could be heard way above the noise of diesel engines and more approaching sirens.

"Noooooooooo, May come back, come back. Somebody save her, please, somebody save her." Her voice rang out above it all, the noise, the sirens, the onlookers who cried also, knowing instinctively there was nothing to be done. Covered with both their blood, she pulled her sister to her own heart and her shrill cries softened with childlike mournful pleas that resounded in the empty air around her. "Help me, somebody please help me."

She'd begged, pleaded, and cried out with a tortured pain of sorrow, the sound of such pure emotional distress stayed with many from that night, but there was no one to save May as she died in her arms. Morgan never let go of her, held her as if she could force her own life into her, force her to come back again, but she lay limp and tattered beyond repair.

When Morgan jolted awake she was in a sweat, she always dreamt it exactly as it happened, wondered why she couldn't at least change its outcome. Wasn't it her nightmare? Didn't she hold that power?

CHAPTER ELEVEN

The third largest city in the state, Juneau, served as Alaska's capital. In the heart of the Tongass National Forest, it was a contrast of sophistication mixed with the beauty of towering mountains that soured above. Miles of scenic trails, tidal beaches and mountains capped by alpine meadows drew people to its stunning beauty.

The state's top attraction was the Mendenhall Glacier, impressive with a face of roughly 100 feet high and 1.5 mile wide. One could visit a bear reserve, thrill in watching a breaching whale, or walk in the serenity and silence of an alpine meadow.

Accessible only by water and air, it was the only state capitol whose governor's mansion sat less than one mile from a prime grizzly bear habitat. It was the grizzly bear habitat that caught Morgan's attention when she read about it. It's what her father had talked about, it's what drew her attention, and maybe if she went there she would find answers.

Stop Morgan, she told herself. There were no answers here, only more questions to why your life turned out the way it did, more reminders of your pain. Morgan armed herself with a wealth of information to plan her day in Alaska's First City. After a confrontation with her mother after breakfast that morning, she was ready for a day alone.

"Mother, you have to be careful, not everyone can be trusted. This isn't the small town of Beach Lake." She'd told her.

Bea looked defensive. "Jerry is a nice man, if you'd give him the time of day you'd know that."

"Men can pose as nice to get themselves into your pocketbook. You're a widow who's comfortable financially, a prime target for scam artists who will work their way into that pocketbook somehow. He befriends you, wheedles his way in with charm, of course that's not the case with Jerry, he has no charm. But you get the idea."

"When did you start judging people?"

"I can see the writing on the wall when you can't," Morgan said.

"Is it so hard to believe that he actually likes me and is not interested in my financial situation?"

Morgan felt bad then, hadn't meant to insinuate it could be the only possibility. "Maybe he does really like you, I just want you to be careful. You've spent the last million years married and things were different back when you were single, I just want you to be aware of what it's like now and what can happen. You're vulnerable."

As much as Morgan would like to think her mother listened to her, she felt she hadn't. She was going to do as she pleased. Morgan had the feeling the roles of mother and child were reversed and saw in her mother the stubbornness of a teenager who thought they knew everything.

"I've been taking care of myself for quite a while now and I think I know what's best for me." Bea smiled when she wanted to shout at her, tell her exactly what came to mind. Which was the fact that Morgan hadn't worried about her before, why was she starting now? "I understand your concern but you don't have to worry, Jerry isn't like that."

"You've only known him a few days, how do you know that?"

Bea knew he had a kind heart and that was enough, she didn't confess the truth that it had actually been longer than a few days. "I guess I can't guarantee anything, but I'll give him the benefit of the doubt. I don't wish to live the rest of my life alone and I'm not saying it will be with Jerry, but I'm saying I'm open to possibilities. If you want to live alone that's your right, but I need people in my life."

Morgan was left with the feeling of guilt for not being in her mother's life. Maybe if she had, Bea wouldn't be so willing to expose herself to outsiders. But did she expect her mother to remain single for the rest of her years? She was still relatively young and she was a very pretty woman, it was only Morgan's sense of loyalty to her father that presumed she would stay single forever.

As she stood outside on the dock now, she watched as her mother and Jerry lazily meandered through town. They smiled, laughed, looked content and Morgan had the feeling she was the outsider instead of the strange man.

"She'll be fine." Ryder said from behind her, saw where her attention was.

"Can I have a guarantee?"

"I think we both know firsthand there's no guarantee's in life." He thought about the changes they'd both suffered through and knew the honesty of his words.

"I've tried to warn her, if she gets hurt at least it won't be on my conscious." There was nothing else Morgan could do because her mother would do as she pleased.

"Find anything?" He motioned toward her handful of brochures and information.

"If I'm supposed to be here to find something, I don't even know where to start looking." She chuckled at the thought, was she supposed to scour strange land looking for something? If so, what?

"I don't think you have to look for it, if you're meant to be here for a reason, it will find you."

Morgan laughed at the absurdity of it. "Should I just stand here and wait? Maybe the ghost of Daddy and May will appear in a cab?"

"If you're going to wait all day, maybe you should stand somewhere out of the way." Ryder teased as he guided her away from the building entrance that had become busy all of a sudden and they stood in the center of the doorway.

"I've never even thought about visiting Alaska, it was always Daddy's dream. Had I had more time I would have done some research and know what to do here. Guess I'll just walk around town."

"What are you trying to decide on?" Ryder asked as he motioned towards the papers and brochures she held.

"The grizzly bears or a whale watching tour. I think I might just go back to bed."

"You have more in you than that."

"I don't think I do."

Ryder saw her eyes before she put her sunglasses on, he knew she'd had a restless night. He'd heard her from his room and it pained him he couldn't get to her to calm her nightmares. He also realized that even if he had, it wasn't him she would want there.

He decided to ask her along anyway. "I know you don't want to be with me, so maybe I shouldn't ask, but I'm going to Admiralty Island. Care to go with me?"

"It isn't that I don't want to be with you, it's…"

Ryder laughed. "You don't have to explain. I don't particularly care to be with you either, but looks like we are, might as well make the best of it."

"Well you don't have to try and persuade me with flattery." She said sarcastically but she too, had to laugh at his honesty.

There was a Tlingit word that meant 'Fortress of the Bears'. Kootznoowoo. The Kootznoowoo Wilderness Area was home to the largest concentration of brown bear in North America, there was approximately one for every square mile of the island. The only way to get there was by kayak, boat or float plane. It was a boat Ryder led her to, but it would be an actual kayak they would take into the park.

"You didn't tell me this part." She immediately began to complain.

"You've already committed now."

"I could back out, couldn't I?" She looked hopeful but saw on his face that he wouldn't let her. "Do I have to go by myself? Can't I go with you?"

"You trust me not to dump you over? You've been awfully mean to me."

"Mean to you? Are you going to throw a fit like you did when I wouldn't play with you when you were eight? You locked yourself in the bathroom for three days."

"You came to see me every day."

"Only because if I didn't you threatened not to play ball with me anymore." Morgan grabbed the oar and got into the small boat.

Ryder didn't say another word as he got in behind her. The air was crisp and clear, she could tell the difference from what she'd been breathing. It was pure. Uncluttered by smog and smoke and she was constantly humbled by surroundings that continued to surprise her.

Morgan wasn't sure what she expected out of Alaska, nor what she would find, but as she looked around to the serene beauty, she wasn't looking for anything in particular, only took in all that it offered. They saw several bears along the shore. Once, as they floated by, one seemed to run towards the water and all she could think was that it would run straight for them. She squealed and almost tipped over the boat.

"Are you trying to tip us over on purpose? Since when were you so scared of something like a bear?"

"He must have been four hundred pounds, probably more."

He laughed at her, wanted to remind her of someone he remembered that wasn't scared of many things, someone who lived life more on the edge, but he was tired of remembering that person, tired of being reminded of someone he no longer knew anymore. Ryder tried not to look at her, tried to distance himself, act as if she were just someone else along on the tour, but how could he do that? There were so many things he instinctively wanted to say or do, things he never would have second guessed before, but they were two other people then, not the people they were now.

They stopped along the shore for awhile and the silence of the vast wilderness was almost deafening. Ironic it was so quiet and yet the scenery spoke in volumes as it engulfed your senses. Clean, crisp air filled your lungs and it was intoxicating to witness such purity, as if you were just then placed on earth as it was built from the beginning.

The beauty of it took Morgan's breath away. Pure, natural, undamaged land untouched and untainted by the hand of man. It belonged to the mountain goats, the bears that frolicked along the shore, and the eagles that took flight overhead. Majestic and proud, it represented the innocence of earth itself. For Morgan it was an emotional experience as she saw what her father dreamt of seeing. In one moment she lost herself in the sheer luxury of the experience, in the next moment her eyes stung with tears for the guilty pleasure.

Ryder watched her take in the splendor that surrounded them, for a moment, maybe a few seconds, he saw no sadness that was ever present in her eyes. For just an instant he saw her let it go, and it was replaced with humbleness. There was something bigger than her, something larger than what she suffered and the brilliance took her mind far from the pain that consumed her. Ryder could only hope it was a feeling she would be able to grasp, carry with her when the week was over. He could only wish for her a healing she needed desperately.

But she'd have to find it again because as quickly as it came, it was gone. He walked towards her and stood quiet. When she finally spoke, her voice was the slightest of whispers.

"You think my father can see this through my eyes somehow?"

"He always said you'd appreciate its beauty. When he talked of Alaska, you talked of the warm and sunny islands, said Alaska wouldn't be on your top ten places to visit. He always knew you'd love it too."

"He always did know me better than I knew myself." She remembered so many times he'd proved that to her in one way or another. "Standing here, seeing what he longed to see one day, it makes me feel guilty."

"He couldn't be here so he sent you. You shouldn't feel guilty because it's what he wanted. Feel satisfied you're fulfilling a wish of his so to speak."

"I try to feel a lot of things, Ryder, I just can't anymore." It was easier to remain numb to anything other than work. The pain was not as great, Morgan thought to herself as she walked away.

They enjoyed the day and when they got back to town Morgan was famished. He took her to a small little place close to the port and they sat at an outdoor table and watched the flow of people, mainly tourists from the ship.

"I think that's Bea, isn't it?" Ryder looked across the street to see Bea coming out of a store. Jerry came behind her and put his arm around her before they wandered on down the sidewalk.

"I can't stand to watch her make a fool of herself."

He looked at Morgan and stopped himself from defending her mother. She knew he'd defend her and spoke again with what she was feeling.

"How can you think that's right? He's going to take advantage of her, break her heart."

"You don't think he could be after your mother for the right reasons? She does have much to offer someone."

"I'm not saying she doesn't, but it certainly isn't him she needs to offer it to." Morgan looked after the two who looked like teenagers as they walked hand in hand.

"I think she's old enough to make that choice."

"But is she smart enough? She's spent years in love with one person, how could she just forget about that?"

"You did," Ryder couldn't stop the words.

"That's different, Ryder, it's not the same."

"No, she didn't have a choice to let go of your father, it was forced on her. You had a choice and you let go. So I guess it is different." He didn't want to say anymore. "I think we've been nice to each other long enough, I can see it's going to get ugly again so I'm going back to the ship."

Why couldn't they just enjoy the day? Enjoy what time they had? Each harbored an anger that came out at the most unexpected times, and they didn't seem to be able to move past it.

Just when Ryder thought the tension between them would ease, it flared up again and he stayed away from her for the rest of the day. As the ship prepared to sail away from Juneau and on to their next stop of Skagway, he stood on the top deck and saw that Morgan had made it back to the ship as he watched her from a distance. She'd dressed for dinner and walked alone then found an empty spot to stand alone. As angry as he was, his heart went out to her still. He'd watched as she gracefully crossed the upper deck, the setting sun behind her. She wasn't the Morgan he remembered from younger days, the one who flippantly and casually went through life with the expectations of everything good. This Morgan was reserved and cautious, life had dealt her a blow she couldn't overcome, and Ryder couldn't help but think of what he'd be like if it had happened to him.

Perhaps he too would have given up on the enchantment of life. For it was what she'd done. Pushed it all aside and went on the straight and narrow without wavering towards anything emotional that could hurt her. She'd been hurt enough. But he also thought of Evan. Maybe that's why she'd come on this trip, she was ready to jump in emotionally now, with him. And she needed this trip to finally put it all behind her.

"Bitter tobacco to chew on, isn't it? To know how something should have been, and how it is?" Jerry was perceptive in his comment, had been informed of their past together.

Ryder looked to Jerry who stood next to him. Bea talked to him, told him of their lives, but Jerry had a knack for picking up on people anyway and would have guessed something between the two.

"I hate to use a cliché' but water under the bridge as they say." Ryder pulled his eyes away from the far off Morgan and glanced elsewhere.

"I'm a big believer in fate. Things happen for a reason, and you two were brought here for a reason."

"Closure? That's about all I see in it."

"Far from closure," he stated. "You two were bound from the beginning of time, can't get away from that, nothing you can do about it."

"Great. So I'll spend the rest of my life pining for a woman I can't have, you've made me feel so much better about it Jerry." There wasn't any sense in not telling him the truth, he had a knack of knowing it anyway.

"Nah, things will work out somehow, have faith."

"I used to have faith, but I've decided I have to give it up for a life instead, I have to exchange it for sanity." Ryder laughed easily and when he spoke again was just as honest and forthright as Jerry as he brought up the knowledge he'd acquired when he'd done his homework on the man. "I happen to know you speak from experience, is that what saw you through the deaths you suffered? Faith?"

The man raised his eyebrows with a quirky smile, surprise in his eyes. "You've done some investigating."

"Bea is very important to me."

"I'm impressed, and glad she has someone that looks out for her, I could have been any old shyster like Morgan thinks I am."

"Bea's vulnerable, but she's smart. She wouldn't have taken up with any old shyster, there's something about you she trusts. On the other hand, I was a little skeptical at first, like Morgan. I had to make sure for my own peace of mind."

"And? Do I pass the test?"

"You're not after her money, that can probably be taken as fact." Ryder laughed casually, he was worth probably billions and the thought of Bea's measly little nest egg compared to that was laughable.

"I learned the hard way money means nothing. Used to be all that drove me, more of it, lot's more of it. How much money does one person need? I'd give away all of it if it meant getting my family back. But I can't buy that with money, so I have little use for it."

"I'm sorry about your family," Ryder said with sympathy in his voice. The horror of losing everyone you loved in one fell swoop was something he couldn't comprehend and Jerry's wife and all of his five children had died in a plane crash.

"It's still a struggle sometimes, but I have to say, this has been the first time I've been able to feel like life could actually move on. I kept telling myself it would, but when I met your Bea, I knew it for sure. I'll never forget my first wife, my first love, but I can see something in Bea that tells me there's another love waiting to be enjoyed."

"Serious so soon?" He knew they'd been enjoying each other, but didn't suspect anything so serious would come out of it.

"Bea will tell you soon enough, but just so you have a heads up, we didn't just meet each other. We've been seeing each other for about six months now. I own the development she just moved into. As I said, I believe in fate. And at my age, I don't believe in wasting precious time, we're granted so little of it." Jerry put his hand on Ryder's shoulder. "You'd be wise to remember that."

His words rung true, Ryder was aware of that, but it was Morgan who needed to understand them, and he couldn't see himself in her life when she finally did come to understand it. She had Evan Berry now. The man he'd met at a conference and Ryder had to admit, he'd liked him, he was a nice guy. It made him that much angrier.

They had a quiet dinner and when Ryder asked where Jerry was, Bea made an excuse for him and Ryder knew it was because of Morgan he wasn't there. Whether it was Jerry's idea or Bea's he wasn't sure, but out of respect for Morgan's feelings, he hadn't joined them.

"Jerry and I are..." Bea began to talk of him and Morgan stopped her.

"I think you're making a fool of yourself, and I don't feel like talking about Jerry. Do you think we could have dinner without mentioning his name?"

"What do you mean making a fool of myself?"

"I saw you two today and you don't know this guy, Mother, yet you're walking down the street holding hands. Don't you read the papers? Don't you watch the news? I'm telling you, he's going to take advantage of you."

Bea looked defiant. "I don't care what you think Morgan, I'm enjoying myself and I'll not have you ruin it."

That evening, it was Bea who left the table early. When she was gone, Ryder rose to leave also.

"So I guess I pissed you off too," Morgan huffed.

"I don't agree with you making Bea so upset. She's trying with you, Morgan, we all are, but you push us away at every turn."

"For as much as you care about my mother, can't you see what's going to happen? Doesn't it worry you?"

"I told you, Bea is old enough to take care of herself. If you were all that worried about her, you would have been there for her all along. Why now?"

"How dare you..."

"If you don't want to include her in your life, that's fine. But don't be upset because she has one."

Ryder left her alone and walked outside for a long time to let the chilly, misty air try and clear his head from thoughts of her, try to take away things he was thinking, things he shouldn't be thinking. He finally retreated to his room long after midnight and just as he was about to lie down, Morgan knocked on the connecting door and he opened it to see her apologetic smile.

"I don't want us to argue, I see no sense in it," she said.

"I don't want to argue either."

Morgan sighed deeply. "I'm fine in Minneapolis, but going back to the house, going back to Beach Lake just brought everything to the surface again."

"Maybe you're not fine in Minneapolis you just hide it better there." He didn't say it meanly but it was the way it was, and he was correct in his assumption.

"You're making me angry again. I don't like to think you still know so much about me."

"I've known you since the day you were born. The surface may change, but the core of you will never really change, I guess I'll always know more about you than probably any other human being on earth."

"Goodnight, Ryder." She closed the door then, it was easy to physically close the door on her past, but it was much harder emotionally.

That night, as he heard her like he had the previous night, Ryder couldn't stop himself from going to her. He checked the door and found she hadn't locked it back and saw her balled up on the bed in a fetal position and in a sweat, the sweat mixed with tears that streamed down her face. She'd never cried when she was awake, but always in her nightmares.

"Shhhh…" He held her to him and wiped her face, rocked her like a frail child in need. "It's okay, Morgan, I'm here with you and it's okay."

He'd been in this position almost every night in between the time after the accident and the time she'd left. It was a role he would have played the rest of his life if need be, had she let him.

"I don't know what to do, Ryder, I don't know what to do." Her voice was a plea for help and he wished he could help her, more than her pain, was his pain in knowing there was nothing he could do.

"Shhhh… It's going to be okay."

"When? When is it going to stop?"

"I don't know, Morgan, I wish I did."

"I still see her face, her bloody face, and…"

"Shhh… It's okay now."

He held her long into the night until she fell asleep again and even when she did, he couldn't let her go. He continued to sit up, leaned against the wall, and she never moved again as he held her in his arms. Coveted her to him for as long as he could, for she would leave again, she always did.

When Morgan woke, still in his strong arms, she didn't move immediately, relished the thought of being there. It surprised her how comforted she felt. Out of the window of the sliding glass doors, she saw more magnificence of the Alaska coastline and saw the quiet morning unfolding before her.

When she did move, he spoke immediately. "You can't move, because I can't move my arms to let you out. Both of them fell asleep hours ago."

She chuckled lightly. "I'm sorry, you could have left me here."

"I could do no such thing, I couldn't move my arms."

Morgan moved slowly, when she was sitting up fully she placed her hands on his shoulders and rubbed down the length of his arms to loosen them again.

"I was waiting for you to move so I could reposition them, but you never did."

"If you weren't so comfortable to lie on, I probably would have moved, so it's your fault."

He finally was able to stretch his arms out. Ryder bent them at the elbows several times. "I'm glad I could oblige. I'll probably be crippled for life, but I'm glad I could oblige."

"You could never throw a baseball very well anyway."

"I always managed to out throw you."

"Who says?" She looked playfully offended.

"So you pitched a season of no hitters your senior year, are you still bragging about it?"

"My season was better than yours that year."

"It was softball." He said as if that were the reason.

"Only because they wouldn't let me on the baseball team."

"They should have, we had a lousy season that year."

"And we won our division," she smiled broadly. "Undefeated State Championship, as a matter of fact."

"They still talk about that season."

Morgan's smile faded and her eyes changed. It was a small town, they still talked about a lot of things. It was why she'd felt so uncomfortable there, still paranoid they talked about her.

Ryder saw the change in her eyes, knew what she was thinking. "They don't blame you, Morgan, it's only you that blames yourself. No one has ever blamed you."

"Death is hard to overcome, no matter that you and mother have made it seem so easy." Her voice was not kind.

She rose then and it amazed him how quickly she could change from one extreme to the next. The tender moment they'd shared was over. He grabbed her arm and stopped her briefly before she could fully escape.

"What are you going to do, Morgan? Spend the next fifty years so wrapped up in death that you forget life?"

"Well I certainly won't be like you and forget death."

"Don't pretend to know how I feel, you didn't stick around to find out." Ryder let her go, didn't care if she left then but she twirled around and faced him.

"And lucky for you I didn't, we'd have probably ended up divorced, maybe I saved us both the headache."

"Why's that? You find out now after all these years together you never wanted what I could give you anyway?"

Morgan wanted him to be as miserable as she, wanted to act as if they'd meant nothing and she could forget it as easily as he had. "What could you give me, Ryder? What did you offer I couldn't get from anywhere else?"

Ryder rose then and stood tall in the room, his presence seemed to fill it, his mood became dark as she saw in his eyes she'd struck a chord and she immediately wanted to retract her words.

"I didn't mean that."

"Maybe you did, this is enlightening and I appreciate the honesty."

He went to leave and she stopped him this time, decided to be honest with what she'd meant, partially honest anyway. "I didn't mean it the way it sounded. I want you to be as miserable as I am. I keep feeling I'm the only one suffering here and I wanted someone else to suffer too. I don't mean to lessen what we shared, that was a low blow." She stepped closer to him then. "When we were kids I would have just thrown something at you and gotten it over with, or physically punched you in the arm. Now I strike with words when you've spent the last hours uncomfortable just to help me get through the night."

He saw the sincerity of her apology. "And a long time ago I was probably guilty in egging you on, I always liked to see you flare up."

She chuckled lightly. "So we're even."

"We could still make out, it always settled it then, you always felt better afterwards."

Morgan playfully punched him in the arm.

CHAPTER TWELVE

The three of them enjoyed breakfast on deck that morning. Bea was anxious to eat and move on with her day but Morgan not as quick to let her.

"I don't know what your plans are, Mother, but I was thinking maybe we could do something together today." Morgan asked the question with a kind of insistence.

"Is that because you really want to do something? Or you don't want me to do anything with Jerry."

"Does it matter…"

"Hey little filly, you coming with us today? I was gonna take Bea…" Jerry walked up then and interrupted.

It infuriated Morgan and she interrupted him. "No, I'm not coming with you today. If your eighth grade education can make you understand, I don't like you."

"You don't have to insult him." Bea defended him and rose.

"She doesn't insult me, Bea, besides, I don't have an eighth grade education, never saw a need to get past the seventh. But I ain't insulted by that." Jerry smiled pleasantly.

Bea didn't say another word as the two left the table. Afterwards, Ryder sat in silence a moment before he spoke.

"Give him a chance?" Ryder said. "I think he's full of good intention."

"The road to hell was paved with good intentions."

"Your mother seems to like him."

"She also used to like seafood, now it makes her sick." Morgan watched as her mother giggled like a school child when Jerry whispered something in her ear. "Aren't they too old for that?"

"Who says love has an age limit?"

"Love? Getting a little ahead of yourself, aren't you? Okay, so maybe she still has desires as a woman, but they have toys for that."

"Speaking from experience?"

Morgan blushed. "I've never needed toys."

"That, I have no doubt." Ryder knew she could have her share of male company any time she so desired. It wasn't something he wished to think about but it crossed his mind that she didn't need anything or anyone else, she had Evan. Why did he have to keep reminding himself of that?

Ryder had begun to instill it in his mind that her anger came from that also. That Evan wasn't here with her. Instead she had him, and it wasn't who she wanted to be with or where she wanted to be.

He could still feel her in his arms as if she lay there, just as she had that morning, just as she had in his dreams over the years without her. Like an imprint of her that wouldn't go away, she was constantly there. He left the table then, needed to be away from her, needed to figure out how he was to get through the rest of the trip when she coursed through his soul like fire.

Bea felt the need to apologize to Jerry when they were alone, apologize for a daughter she didn't know anymore. "I'm sorry about Morgan, I don't know what's gotten into her."

"What she's gone through is too much for a strong stappin' farm hand to carry around on his back, much less a little ole' thing like her."

"I've tried over the years but she shut herself off and won't let anyone in. As much as it upset me when she moved away I thought after the fact maybe it would be best for her, but even that hasn't helped. I don't know what to do for her. I don't know what she needs to be able to get through this. I'm beginning to think she never will."

"Maybe I'll talk to her."

Bea looked concerned with his statement. "I don't know, Jerry, I don't think Morgan..." She hesitated, how could she say it politely? "I don't think she's comfortable with you yet."

"Doesn't hurt my feelings Bea, you can say it, Morgan doesn't like me. I know that, but whether she likes me or not, I wouldn't turn my back if I could help her."

"How could you help her?" It almost hurt her feelings for him to think her own mother could do nothing and he could just swoop in and make everything okay.

"Mind if I don't spend the day with you? Maybe I'll take a crack at Morgan. There's something that might be able to help a little."

She wasn't sure what he thought he could do, but she obliged. "It can't hurt."

"If we're not back on the ship tonight, don't worry. We'll be back on it sometime tomorrow."

"Tomorrow? We're not in port tomorrow, we're sailing through Glacier Bay."

"We'll get back to this big ole' boat somehow, in the meantime, don't worry, she'll be safe."

She watched after him and her brief minute of worry subsided. She trusted him to look out for her. How he was going to get her to go anywhere with him, Bea wasn't sure because Morgan seemed to hate him. If he could, he would probably have to sell his soul to the devil. It surprised her to think he would do that for her and for Morgan who appeared to hate him. Then again it didn't surprise her at all, it was the type of man he was, underneath all the costume and persona of a big tough man lie a heart of gold.

****

"Hey little filly."

Morgan had been standing on the dock and huffed at his interruption and turned away from him. "How many times do I have to repeat myself, I really don't like for you to call me that."

"You don't like quite a bit about me, but I can't change the way I am. I won't change the way I am."

"That's too bad." She turned away from him and continued down the street. "Why are you following me? Did my mother come to her senses and ditch you?"

"I thought we'd spend the day together."

Morgan laughed cynically. "We? As in you and I? You can't be serious."

"Serious as a brander with a hot iron in his hand."

"I'm perfectly content to spend my day without you."

"I could rope you up like a calf and drag you through the streets here, but I tell you what, I'll make you a deal."

She stopped and faced him then. "What do you want, Jerry?"

"Come with me today, and when the sun comes up tomorrow, if I steered you wrong and you're still mad at me, I'll leave your mother alone."

"What are you talking about? What is this all about?"

"I want to help you, Morgan."

She laughed. "How do you think you could possibly help me with anything? I don't need help, and if I did, I certainly don't need any help from you."

"Just trust me today, what have you got to lose?"

She looked at him for a long time, this garish man in his Halloween clothes. As the sun glinted off the rhinestones of his jacket, she caught something in his eye, something odd that told her to trust him.

Jerry could see her hesitation. "And what kind of a deal is that? You'd pass up your chance of gettin' rid of me? If you feel the same about me tomorrow, I'll leave Bea alone. Now that should be worth your time right there."

It was quiet between the two when Jerry placed her in a helicopter and they took off over the land. Massive amounts of untouched, unspoiled land that passed below them. The helicopter easily skimmed the tops of trees, so close she thought she could touch them. She watched as a pod of whales played below them, the pilot hovered so they could watch as long as possible and when she saw one breach the water she audibly gasped at the sight to behold.

It was nature's playground, the beginning of time, a society all its own that didn't need machines, technology, or any other thing mankind could offer it. It didn't need anything to exist and that fact was monumental and obvious in pristine glory. How long they were in the air, Morgan wasn't sure, she was engrossed with it all. As if she was by herself and Jerry not even present. Then they landed in a pristine mountain top along a serene lake.

"We'll be having lunch and staying for awhile, you go ahead and refuel." Jerry instructed the pilot and he took off again.

Morgan looked around at the still wilderness and didn't see a thing in sight and thought he'd lost his mind. "Having lunch? You aren't going to tell me I have to kill it myself, are you? Are we supposed to hunt for it or something?"

"We could, but don't suppose you'd take kindly to it. This way," he answered and began to walk and she followed.

She still didn't see anything or anywhere they could be headed to as they were surrounded by woods, the alpine lake and a field. But he led her behind a group of trees and a house was revealed that hadn't been seen before because it blended in so well with its surroundings. The door opened before they reached it and a small boy came out followed by a man and a woman. The boy ran to him immediately with arms spread wide.

"Grandpa."

"Hey little fella," Jerry easily picked the boy up.

The woman looked to Morgan with surprise, expected Bea that she'd heard so much about, but couldn't believe this young woman would be her. "This isn't…"

"No, this isn't Bea, this is actually her daughter."

She smiled broadly and gave Morgan a welcome hug. "It scared me for a minute, I didn't want to think Jerry was picking up women closer to my age than his own. It's so nice to meet you. Where's your mother? I thought she was coming?"

"I…" Morgan stammered, she didn't know why her mother hadn't been there, didn't know what she was doing there.

"Change of plans and she didn't come. You'll meet her soon enough."

"I'm Dana." The woman introduced herself then everyone else. "And this is my husband Brad and our son Chandler."

"Nice to meet you," Morgan said, immediately felt welcome in their presence.

They made her comfortable. They all enjoyed a delicious meal and afterwards she sat on the porch with Dana and enjoying a great cup of coffee while Jerry, Brad and Chandler fished at the lake.

"I was so looking forward to meeting Bea. It's been a long time since Jerry's had an important woman in his life."

Morgan was confused, how could she know about them? How could this strange woman who lived on a mountain in Alaska know about someone Jerry had just met? Then it was revealed they'd been seeing each other for much longer than Morgan knew about. And for a moment it hurt her feelings, saddened her that this strange woman would know more about her mother than Morgan did.

But she couldn't be angry with anyone but herself, her mother hadn't shared this with her because Morgan hadn't let her. Like everything else, she'd pushed her out of her life and didn't blame Bea for not wanting to open up with her. Morgan had never given her the chance nor indicated she'd want her to.

"He was so excited when he met her. I'm so glad Bea got to know him, he's a little hard to take at first, but once you get to know Jerry, there's no one else like him."

"You're right about that." Morgan looked out to the man whose rhinestones glinted in the sun. She was right about no one else being like him, as for getting to know him, she wasn't sure, but what she knew of him so far was odd.

"I'm so glad to meet you, and it gives me a little more time to prepare for Bea. He said this trip would only be for the day, but they planned to come next month and spend a few weeks."

Again, it dawned on her how little she knew of her mother's life. The trip hadn't been a ploy, she had no doubt her father had planned it, but it was all strange that Jerry came out of nowhere. Was it another sign of some kind? A strange man her mother had a relationship with who would also have ties to Alaska? Morgan was confused even more.

Dana continued to talk when Morgan seemed lost in thought somewhere. "Jerry can't wait for her to meet Chandler. His grandson is like nothing else in his eyes."

"So you're his daughter?" It was still unclear her relationship to Jerry, but for Chandler to be his grandson, Dana was either his daughter, or Brad his son.

"I was his daughter in law."

"Was? Oh, so you're divorced from his son and married Brad?"

"No, my husband, Jerry's son, was killed." She said it softly, thought Morgan would have known.

"Oh I'm sorry. I didn't know. I really just met Jerry a few days ago."

"He was killed along with the rest of Jerry's family in a plane crash."

"His whole family?" Morgan asked incredulously.

"His wife and all five of his children, they were coming here to see our son as a matter of fact."

"I... I didn't know."

Dana went on to explain the circumstances. They were all at Jerry's home in Texas when she went into labor early. He piled them all in a plane and at the last minute, had to take care of some things first and was taking a commercial flight rather than their private jet. The plane went down on a foggy night, the weather was to blame. Chandler Sr., her husband, had been his oldest child at thirty five, then it ranged down to his youngest who was only eleven, around the same age as Chandler Jr. was now. And they were all from the same wife, he hadn't been married several times, he and Ruth had married young and in love till the day she died, even long after.

The news shocked her. "He lost everyone."

"Everyone except Chandler Jr. He was born less than two hours after his father died. It's all he had left and if he hadn't of had Chandler Jr. to live for I'm not sure what would have happened to Jerry."

Morgan watched the little boy who wouldn't know his father or the extended family of his grandmother and aunts and uncles. Her own father had been the one to shape her life, an integral part of who she was. Then she thought of Dana's words. 'If he hadn't of had Chandler Jr. to live for...' A child helped Jerry find life again, a child who depended on him, someone who would look to him for answers and guidance. Morgan felt her own guilt all over again of what she'd been doing to her mother, shut her out, in turn Bea had Ryder to turn to. Without that, she shuttered to think what would have become of her.

She and Dana talked well into early evening and when the helicopter landed to pick them up, Morgan thought they would be going back to the ship, but that was not the case.

"Shouldn't we be getting back?" She questioned when they seemed to be going further into the mountains.

"We'll get back tomorrow."

"Tomorrow?"

"What you need to see we may have to wait all night on, so we'll go back tomorrow."

When the helicopter landed again, it left them with plenty of supplies such as food and hot coffee, Jerry was prepared as he made a fire and brewed the coffee from an old tin pot he'd packed from Dana's house.

"You seem to be experienced in this wilderness thing." Morgan said as she watched him use expert skill, admitted only to herself she was a little nervous about living off the land for the night.

"Love it here. Nothing like living off the land, it's what God intended. Tons of things to eat and survive on, some folks have to, won't be a McDonalds around the next mountain."

His words struck her. Her father had mentioned Alaska not being commercialized, had mentioned the fast food chain specifically and a chill ran up her spine.

"Did I say something?" He looked up to see her strange expression.

"No," Morgan answered softly, it was coincidence, all coincidence.

Night fell and they sat in the dark. He made sure she was comfortable with a warm blanket and she bundled inside of it and listened to the sounds of the wilderness. She wasn't sure what was expected of her, but she sat in the silent, still, black of night and waited for something. What they waited on, Morgan wasn't sure, but Jerry insisted they sit.

"Is this to make me feel even guiltier than I already do?" Morgan finally spoke to break the silence.

"How's that? How's sitting here on this mountain doing nothing, making you feel guilty?"

"It's where my father should be, and because of me, he isn't. This was his trip, I never wanted to be here, I wanted to be in the islands."

"But he sent you here." Jerry said with an even tone, a knowing tone. "Why else do you think you're here?"

"Because it's what my mother wanted."

"You don't think your father and sister sent you here?"

"How ridiculous is that?" She didn't acknowledge she thought he was right.

"The Lord sends you places you need to be, that's why you're here, there's something here you need to see or need to do. I can't tell you what it is cause' I don't know, but you'll find it or it will find you. Keep your eyes open."

She looked at him as if his words were truth, odd he would know exactly what she'd been feeling. "How do you know he sent me here?"

"They've been giving you signs, he and May, and you've been trying to ignore them."

"How do you know about any signs?" Her full attention was to him now, as if this odd man had direct insight.

"I've been there Morgan. I've been where you are." He paused and went on. "My entire family hounded me with things before they gave me a heart attack and woke me up."

"I'm sorry about your family, but I can't believe they gave you a heart attack. Maybe that was all the steak you live off of."

He laughed, she didn't offend him. "It all comes together and we know. Little things we pay no mind to, then all of a sudden they make sense, and we know it's them."

"I don't know it's them. It's preposterous to think."

"That's why you're miserable and you'll stay miserable if you don't wake up."

Morgan became defensive, buried herself deeper into the blanket and didn't feel like she needed to open up to this stranger, one who pretended to know her so well.

"You can't stop it, they'll keep coming at you and you're being selfish not to listen to them and not to see the signs. They can't be ignored."

"How am I being selfish?" Morgan didn't like the accusation.

"You're not letting them go, you're not setting them free." Jerry moved closer to her, placed himself directly beside her on the ground. "What kind of signs have you been having?"

Morgan hesitated for a moment then answered the question. "A few little things."

"Little things? That's why you've been missing them if that's the way you look at them. You know they're signs, you just don't want to admit it."

"Coincidences, I call them coincidences," she said.

"You call them something, so at least you recognize they exist. They're as large as a big ole' grizzly standing right in front of you, tell me about your 'coincidences'."

Morgan's voice was soft as she revealed the things she'd been thinking about. "The words of God's will, they keep coming back to me in one form or another. It's what May said to me as she lay dying in my arms."

Jerry had been told the story, but he hadn't realized, and hadn't put it together, that her sister actually died in her arms. "I often thought when my family left me that I should have been there with them. But then I came to see that had I been there, and been the one to survive, I couldn't have watched while they died. It's one thing to go on after a death, it's another to actually witness death."

"It haunts me every night but her words keep coming back, I heard them from a patient and it was her voice, it was May who said them. I think I'm just losing my mind."

Jerry laughed lightly. "You're not losing your mind. I know there's more to the puzzle, you just have to put the pieces together. What other things have happened?"

"The timing of Evan seeing Ryder, right as my mother was selling our home, and bringing him to the surface of my thoughts. Two people who don't know each other, two strangers, and yet how odd they would meet. How strange a coincidence is that?"

"Another sign you didn't want to see."

"It's all strange, mysterious, coincidence. Just like Desiree mentioning May's spirit, and then me seeing it in the brochure for Alaska. Words written across a brochure that told me to find my spirit in Alaska." Morgan lay her head down on the tops of her knees and buried her face in the blanket as she thought about the ballerina, her sister's words that said she would dance to the ballerina again. She couldn't, Morgan couldn't dance anymore. "I can't find her, Jerry, she's not here, it's all bull crap and I keep reading something into it."

Jerry looked at her for a long time. "There's a big sign there I know. You've seen her, haven't you? You've seen your sister."

"It was the reflection of the sun." She tried to shrug it off but couldn't. The look on her sister's face made her choke back the tears. "She blames me too. I saw it in her face, in the window of her room when I went back home for the first time. She had a sad look on her face, she blames me."

"It wasn't blame you saw, think about it long and hard, she's sad for you, she's trying to help you."

It was ridiculous to sit on this hill with an odd strange man and think she was going to find something in stupid signs. She didn't want to think about the pain that seemed unbearable to her now. She'd been sitting and concentrating on them, talking about them and the anguish had overtaken her yet again. She wanted to leave, get away from Jerry, from Alaska, from the memory of killing them.

Sitting on this mountain and rehashing it all wasn't making anything better. Jerry only meant for it to torture her, he was getting back at her for all the mean things she'd said to him. Morgan's thoughts were denial that there were no signs, she didn't actually believe it, but she wasn't sure what to believe anymore.

Morgan had to choke back her tears. "What am I supposed to take from all this? It doesn't take away the accident, it doesn't take away my blame and responsibility for their deaths. It's like living through it again, so what good is it doing to try and read things in coincidental signs?"

"It means they're trying to tell you something."

Morgan looked at this man and wanted to believe his words but she wanted him to tell her what it all meant, wanted him to fix everything. Isn't that why he brought her there? Wasn't he trying to help her somehow? Then take away the pain, she wanted to scream. The guilt of killing them, the guilt of sitting in Alaska on a trip that was her fathers dream, and he not there to see it.

"They're trying to tell me not to forget it. They're trying to make me remember for the rest of my life. Well, they don't have to worry about that, I'm tortured every day. And I'm sorry, I'm so sorry." Morgan began to cry, her tears flooded out and she couldn't stop them.

Other than her nightmares, it had been the first time she'd cried since it happened. She hadn't cried at the funeral, hadn't cried afterwards, and hadn't cried when she left her home never to return. In that one moment, high on a mountain in the wilds of Alaska, it all streamed out. Her sobs echoed in the distance in the lonely still night. She wasn't sure how long she cried as an old garish cowboy held her in his arms. An unexpected shoulder to cry on, one that didn't blame or judge her.

It was a shoulder that seemed to offer her something no one else ever had, an unencumbered place of solace, he hadn't known her father and twin sister, Morgan hadn't taken them from him so there was no presumed guilt and blame she always placed upon herself, unlike the way she felt for taking loved ones from her mother and Ryder. She was surprised to find herself in the arms of a man she didn't even like, and she handed over her burden easily, cried and felt a reprieve as he held her.

It was a long time before Jerry spoke, his simple word was whispered into the silence of the dark. "Look."

Morgan looked up to find a faint glow on the dark horizon. A greenish light that formed an arch and stretched lazily across the broad sky, then additional bands of light formed, seemed to drift overhead and float above it all, waved as if a gentle breeze guided it.

"Oh my God," her words were choked with quiet emotions and tears.

"Northern lights, sounds simple enough, but legend is, it's the dance of the dead. Spirits of the dead on their way to heaven. It's a beautiful sight, isn't it? There's no pain in death, not any pain for those who've passed, only for those left behind."

Suddenly, everything looked bigger and brighter as colors filled the sky. A reddish tint, then blues and purples appeared and it began to move faster as if it danced to music all its own. Bright points of light swirled overhead as the entire sky filled with color and motion, took on something magical and Morgan was transfixed, unable to move or breathe as she watched, captivated by the astounding phenomenon.

It transformed before her, the sky was streaked with brilliant hues of color. A sight that took her breath away, one that hypnotized her as she watched a spiral dance of magnificent beauty as the celestial atmosphere came alive. Morgan was mesmerized by the glowing curtain of light forms as it waved and danced towards heaven. As it began to fade she became desperate, looked to the sky and tried to see their faces before the lights faded and disappeared. Her father's face, May's face, she searched desperately for them, frantically, before it was all gone. But as hard as she tried to imagine it, she couldn't see them there.

Her words were a whisper of realization. "They're not there."

"No, Henry and May aren't there tonight. They can't leave for awhile. They can't leave you, Morgan, they'd never leave you in a time of need. Once you let them go, they can be free too."

"I don't know how to let them go. What are they trying to tell me, Jerry? What are they trying to do?"

"There's life out there little filly, and if you don't live... you die. May not be the real death where you're put in the ground and a priest prays over you, but emotionally dead is just as bad. What's the point in not being buried?" Jerry's next words gave her some sort of answer she sought. "They're trying to help you live, take their hand Morgan, and let them guide you back."

She looked at Jerry with a blank expression. It was the only thing that seemed to make sense to her, out of all the confusion of her heart and mind, his words broke through something and made sense. The signs, all the signs that led her to this place, led her to her mother, to Ryder, to Alaska and even to Jerry. All the signs had been real. She now only had to grasp them, to covet them to her and let them help.

The brilliant light before her was something from another world. It seemed alive and breathing, pulsed with life. In one instant, something of her pain eased. It was the smallest of release, but a little of her burden she carried was chipped away, a little of her heart opened. Just the tiniest bit, but it was a beginning.

CHAPTER THIRTEEN

At dinner that evening, Ryder had been looking forward to seeing Morgan since he hadn't all day. He hadn't heard her in her room, hadn't seen her about town or on the ship and it surprised him how anxious he'd been to see her face. But when he arrived, it was only Bea who was ready to order the meal immediately.

"Aren't we going to wait for Morgan?" Ryder asked.

"I'm pretty sure they missed the boat."

"Missed the boat?" His eyebrows rose in shock and surprise. "They? Who's they?"

"Jerry told me that whatever happened, not to worry. He also told me it may not be till tomorrow that I'd see them again." She looked to the waiter and began to order. "I'd like..."

"And you're not worried about this? No offense Bea, you may like the guy and all, but he is a stranger. And you let him basically kidnap Morgan to take her... God knows where. We're in the middle of Alaska." If he sounded harsh he hadn't meant to, but worry took hold.

"She'll be fine, and it wasn't a kidnapping." Bea chuckled, took it so lightly.

"You hardly know him, how can you think this is okay? Morgan doesn't even like him, why would she willingly go off with him?"

"I'm not sure how willing she was, but she went." Then she saw in his eyes how frightened he actually was and reached across the table for his hand. "Ryder, calm down. It will be okay, I promise. I know I don't know him well, but I trust Jerry. I don't know why, something about him makes me feel comfortable, he doesn't mean her any harm if that's what you're worried about."

Ryder didn't calm down, but he did order something for dinner, wouldn't have been able to tell anyone later because he couldn't remember exactly what it was, but he knew he'd probably ordered more drinks than he should have. Even that didn't calm him. After dinner he declined Bea's invitation to join her and some others for the show and headed straight for the internet cafe'. He wasn't sure that even if he found anymore information on Jerry there was anything he could do with it.

The internet told him basic things, wouldn't reveal that as far as Ryder knew he took an Alaskan cruise every other week just to pull someone off the ship and take them to some remote, desolate location in the colds of the mountain and keep them a slave forever, possibly sold his victims on some kind of black market or fed them to the bears for kicks. All kinds of crazy thoughts ran through his mind and he didn't know what to think.

He'd already discovered his financial stability but there was nothing to tell him about the man's emotional stability. You could be one of the richest people in the world, and it appeared he was, but that didn't mean you couldn't be a psychopath killer.

As much as he tried, quite a few drinks in his attempt, Ryder couldn't relax and stop worrying. Horrid visions ran through his head as he tossed and turned late into the night until early morning when he finally gave up, ordered pots of coffee and sat on his balcony until the sun started to rise. Then he made his way onto the top deck and paced there.

Few people milled about and he saw no sign of Morgan and Jerry as Ryder paced the deck back and forth. All kinds of things continued to run wild through his mind and he couldn't stop the worry and concern he felt, it only had time to escalate to dangerous proportions. How could Bea have trusted the stranger? Of all the cons and ploys people pulled in the world for deceit and evil, and she'd trusted an overgrown cowboy she really knew nothing about. He'd trusted him too, how could he have been so foolish?

They hadn't returned the evening before, and as the ship sailed through Glacier Bay he continued to look around in the hopes of seeing them. But how were they to return? The ship was sailing through the bay, when were they going to return? The next day at port? Ryder couldn't wait that long, would call out the National Guard and every branch of the military service, all the armed forces, long before then.

He'd done his research. Jerry was on the Forbes list of richest people, owned half of Texas and his investments had been kind to him, very kind. An archived article online featured his home, a massive stone and wood structure of more than twenty thousand square feet and there were more pictures of his family and another article about the plane crash they'd periled in.

Jerry wasn't looking for a free ride on Bea's little nest egg, but that meant nothing. Something could have happened to them, anything could have happened, they could be lost in Alaska, in the many forests, on a glacier and were suffering hypothermia, they could have been attacked by bears.

Morgan had suffered so much, the last thing she needed was another devastating blow, and he would blame himself if something happened to her. He would carry the guilt for the rest of his life, just as she had done. He thought of all that could happen, maybe Jerry was part of some wife selling ring, slave selling ring. He could take her up into the wilds of Alaska and no one would ever be able to find her. He could... as the thoughts were about to escalate even more, he saw a helicopter in the distance and watched as it made its way to the ship and landed high above, a few moments later, after dropping off passengers, it left again.

Then across the way on the deck he saw the glint of sun off Jerry's rhinestone embedded jacket he'd worn the previous day. The man was like a circus clown that headed a parade.

Ryder rushed towards them and his voice was heavy with concern and anger. "Where the hell have you been?"

"Morning, Ryder," Morgan answered calmly.

When she smiled up at him a rush of something strange ran through every blood vessel. She was different, not the same person she was the day before, he could see it in her smile, her eyes, the way she touched his arm nonchalantly.

Jerry patted him on the shoulder. "Calm down young buck, Alaska is too beautiful for you to be so tense."

Ryder could only stare at him, mystified to what had taken place between them. Was it some sort of Stepford wives transformation? He'd cloned her and this was a copy? His concerns still hovered around the edge of crazy hysteria, and maybe he would never know exactly, but in one instant as he looked deep into Morgan's eyes, it didn't matter much anymore.

There was a glitter there, a tiny brief glimpse into the past when all was well with the world. Maybe she wasn't fully back yet, but it was the first sign he'd seen since the accident that indicated she could possibly be on her way. He tried to think of a way to have her physically examined to make sure she wasn't a science experiment duplicate.

Jerry smiled broadly. "Your little filly is fine, back safe and sound in one piece."

Ryder looked to Morgan again and the look on her face took another moment to register, there was a soft smile that was real, a soft face that wasn't as hard around the edges. Ryder didn't know what happened to them that night, and probably never would, but he thanked God silently for the small glimpse of a woman he once knew.

Jerry smiled in his usual broad way. "I'll see you two later, there's a woman I have to see."

"I'm too tired for breakfast, tell Mama I'll see her at dinner?" Morgan called out to him and hadn't noticed the word she used until Ryder mentioned it.

"Mama? I've always like the sound of that, I just never thought I'd ever hear you say it again."

"I hadn't even realized. What are you doing out here so early in the morning?"

He looked at her and laughed. She hadn't known the torment he'd been through all night, hadn't suspected he'd spent his night in a hell he couldn't shake himself out of. His words were said casually with a light laugh of release. "Just wandering around, getting an early jump on the day."

She looked at him, knew he'd worried about her and hadn't slept at all. "It's nice that you worried."

"I did some homework on Jerry and thought I was comfortable with what I'd found, but it was a little different when he takes you off into the wilderness and doesn't return," he smiled sheepishly.

"When did you do homework on Jerry? When did you know about him?"

"Before last night," he answered her honestly, no point in trying to pretend he hadn't.

"I found out quite a bit about Jerry. You could have given me a heads up. I'd been accusing him of wanting my mothers little nest egg when he carries that much around for spending money. You let me embarrass myself, why didn't you tell me?"

"Figured you'd find out soon enough."

"I can't believe you knew it! You knew it and let me make a fool of myself, the whole time laughing behind my back, how could you?" Her hand playfully swatted him across the shoulder.

"I used you for entertainment, it was so funny I couldn't help myself. Plus it also served to give me more insight, made me realize how humble and nonchalant Jerry was about his wealth. Whenever you insulted him with your hillbilly innuendos he never acted as if it weren't true. I liked the way he let you assume what you wanted about him." Ryder looked towards him as he made his way across the deck. "The man has character."

"But you let me make an ass of myself."

"I had nothing to do with that, you did that on your own. Besides," he paused for a moment before he continued. "I also liked the way you worried about your mother. He at least woke you up a little, if it weren't for Jerry you may have been lost in your own little world and not paid attention to her."

She couldn't argue, everything he said was true and she had no defense to offer. "Ryder, I called him a... never mind, it gives me a headache to think about it."

Morgan looked out to the new day that was beginning, she had a ways to go, but she could feel herself already being pulled back. They stood silently a few moments until she spoke again.

"I'm sorry, Ryder."

"For worrying me? I was half out of my mind, I thought…"

Morgan placed her hand on his arm and stopped him, she could still see a little of the fear in his eyes. "I'm sorry for everything. For the way I've been acting on this trip, for the way I've been pushing you and mother away from me," she paused before she continued. "I'm sorry for everything."

Again, he wondered how they'd spent their night, but he would never know, and oddly enough, he didn't feel a need to know. Morgan was on her way back, not to him, but he would deal with that again, just as he'd done the first time she'd left him. More important, she was on her way back to the living, she could possibly begin to heal now.

Since neither of them had any sleep the evening before, each retreated back to their rooms to watch the glaciers passing from their balcony as they sailed through the bay. Morgan felt the mist on her face, the cold, damp misty rain that was a constant. It was as if it was sent from the clouds directly to her, Angel mist that fell upon her face, as if it were dew from heaven to wake her from the long tormented sleep.

It invigorated her, rejuvenated her. She felt like a long dormant rose that lay buried in the cracked, dry, ground and simply needed the nourishment of water to bloom again. Morgan let it refresh her, took from it the comfort it offered. Alaska passed before her and with each passing ripple of wave, she let the pain ease out of her slowly, didn't try to hold onto it when it wanted to leave her.

She saw no one that day. Alone and content in a solitude she needed to piece together the signs and gain meaning, to try and understand what was being asked of her, what they needed from her. Morgan came to the realization there was nothing she had to do, her heart filled with a knowledge they were trying to lead her back. All she had to do was let them.

She woke from a restful sleep and realized she would possibly be late for dinner. She rushed to get ready and took a quick moment to give one final look in the mirror, and when she did, she stared for a long time. So much, that her focus made everything else disappear and become a blur, everything but the face that stared back.

To her astonishment, it was no longer May she saw, her sister was gone and in its place was Morgan. She reached up and touched her cheek, after all this time she finally saw herself again.

"Oh, May. Do you have to go?" Her words were whispered to a silent, empty room. "Just because I find myself, does that mean I have to lose you again?"

****

That evening, they all met for dinner as planned and Jerry was included. Morgan smiled at her mother and bent to kiss her.

"Don't think I ain't waitin' for my own over here." Jerry commented. "Come on little filly, you know you want to kiss me too."

His pet name that had previously infuriated her, made her laugh now. To the surprise of both Ryder and her mother, Morgan bent and kissed him too then took his napkin out of his shirt and placed it on his lap. "If you have to eat steak, then at least eat it properly," she teased.

His clothes loud and obnoxious, his mannerisms left something to be desired at times, and his ability to say whatever came to his mind was something he never held back on. But as Morgan looked to this improper man she'd judged before, she now looked at with new respect.

Not because of the money she'd discovered he'd had, not because he was wealthy and powerful, but because he'd overcome the death of his entire family and was willing to help her do the same. Willing to share with her, even when she'd been so nasty to him, something she wouldn't have been able to find on her own.

Bea was silent as she watched the two interact. She looked to Ryder who had the same expression as the two previous adversaries teased each other with playfulness. Jerry wanted four of the biggest steaks they could 'wrastle' up and Morgan changed his order to two and a large salad.

"I'm a doctor, it will clog your arteries and…" She wanted to remind him of his heart attack he'd had, the one he talked about briefly but she wasn't sure if her mother knew everything about him and felt it was something Jerry should reveal, not her.

"You're a baby doctor, and I don't plan on birthin' no babies. All I want is a few steaks. Big, red, juicy, meat steaks, none of that soy or vegetable burger stuff."

"I may be a 'baby doctor', but I'm still qualified to tell you that the way you eat isn't good for you." Morgan sipped her water and looked defiant.

"Ryder's a doctor too, and he'll probably eat four."

Ryder certainly wasn't going to defy her. "Only when Morgan isn't looking, I'll stick to one for now."

"Maybe we should have come on our own, this little thing wants to starve me." Then he turned his attention back to Morgan. "Maybe you should have four, put some meat on those bones. Need some meat to weigh you down on a bull."

"I don't plan on being on a bull."

"I have one in Texas, when you come you can ride it. But we'll have to fatten you up first, you'd fly off quicker n' I can flick a dragonfly." Jerry smiled to Bea. "Bea here is gonna ride too."

Bea was still dumbfounded by what was happening before her, was almost in tears as she watched her daughter. Morgan smiled, a genuine smile that shone on her face. It wasn't a constant, but she caught a glimpse of the girl that used to be when she least expected it. She'd been assured by both Jerry and Ryder that Morgan was back safe and sound, but neither had told her anything else and she hadn't seen her daughter all day. Now, as she looked to her face, she truly saw the beginnings of the daughter she used to know, not the one she'd become.

"Tell her, Bea, tell her you plan on bull riding."

"If my mother rides a bull, I'll ride a bull." Morgan said the words but didn't think Bea would even consider the notion.

"We can have matching boots and spurs." Then Bea looked worried. "Do you wear boots and spurs on a bull?"

"Darlin', you can wear anything you want on a bull." Jerry openly flirted and Bea blushed.

Morgan almost spit out her water when she laughed. "Okay, that's more than I can take, I'll not think of the two of you... never mind."

Ryder commented also. "I think another topic of dinner conversation might be more appropriate. Does anyone know what the show is tonight?"

They laughed and talked through dinner. After two steaks, Jerry wanted another but had dessert instead.

"I don't know what happened, it's amazing." Bea mentioned to Jerry later when they were on their own, she was dumbfounded at the turnaround she'd witnessed.

"She'll find her way, I'm sure of it. That little filly won't be able to hold back now, I'm not saying it will happen overnight, but she'll be back to you, she's trying."

"What happened out there?"

Jerry looked towards the silence of Alaska. "She just needed a little guidance to find what she's been needin' to find, something she's been looking for. I just pointed her in the right direction."

It was all he said on the subject, and all he ever would say. It wasn't important she saw the northern lights, it wasn't important where they were or what they'd done. What was important was what she took away from it, and that was something intangible. Something she would have to keep inside herself and carry with her to see herself the rest of the way through.

After dinner, Ryder watched from a distance as Morgan laughed and smiled among a small group of women. They were friends her mother had met and they'd talked her into having a hot toddy with them. He watched as a small transformation was taking hold. What happened last night, carried over to that evening, and he was happy for her. It still bothered him that it still wouldn't mean anything to him, but he was happy for her. He turned and left.

"Why didn't you join us? Harmless little old ladies, you could have joined us for a drink." Morgan said from behind him.

"Harmless? You should have seen them last night when they got up on stage and danced with the production show."

Morgan laughed easily, stood next to him along the banister and looked out to the wonder of nature. "Maybe that's why I like them, they're not afraid to live a little."

"You used to be that way," he commented with true sincerity. It was something about her he'd always loved.

"Maybe I will again, who knows what's in store for me now?"

"Guess we never know what life has in store for us."

"I couldn't have imagined it, but this trip has done me some good, and I'm not even sure what it is."

"We don't let go of things till we're ready, it can't be forced on us." Ryder's words not only insinuated her letting go, but him as well. "Guess you were ready."

Morgan wanted hope from him, hope that he hadn't fully let go of her. "You seem to be doing well, is life the way you expected it to be?"

"It's about the farthest thing I ever expected for myself, but guess that's something I have to live with. You didn't give me a choice to do otherwise." He wanted her to know it was through no fault of his own.

"You found someone else." She brought up the subject of Stella.

He looked at her with curiosity, wondered what she spoke of. "What are you talking about?"

"Desiree told me about Shelley, Sheila? Whatever her name is. Said you were living with her, and were going to be married."

"She did, did she?" Ryder thought of the statement, and laughed to himself. Let her think what she would, even if it wasn't true, it still wouldn't matter. And he would sound pathetic if he'd told her he hung on for all that time in the hopes of her coming back to him. She had Evan now, why shouldn't she think he'd found someone also?

Morgan waited but he didn't tell her about the woman, he didn't open up and talk like they used to before they committed themselves to one another after several failed attempts to date others. "Does she know how much peanut butter and jelly she'll go through?"

Morgan knew that about him, it was his favorite sandwich and he ate it all the time, or used to. She knew many things about him at one time, what did she know about him anymore? He could have changed and could be a completely different person now.

She spoke again. "It's still your favorite, isn't it?"

"It's the easiest thing in the world to fix."

"I have a feeling when you have children you'll have to buy it by the case."

It struck him she talked of his life with the notion she wouldn't be in it. Maybe subconsciously it was the message she wanted to get across. If he needed any of his own signs, he took that as one of them to indicate she had no plans on being in his life.

"I'll buy stock in the companies." He said with a short tone.

"Does Stella want lots of children?" She used her correct name that time, he hadn't corrected her before, and she wanted him to know she actually knew it.

"Why are we talking about Stella?"

"We used to talk about others. Remember that period of time we tried to date others and it didn't work? I thought..."

"Well I don't think it's something we can do now. I won't ask you about Evan and you don't ask about Stella." He lashed out at her when she offered friendship, but he was jealous Evan would be the one to reap the rewards of her healing.

"Evan and Ray said they met you." She remembered the story Ray told her, the hopes he had for them. She wanted to explain that it was merely a friendship, an innocent companionship that would never move past what it was.

"At a conference," he said.

"Ray's been a great friend, and..." She still had the urge to explain more but he stopped her.

"I'm glad you found someone, and so have I. Let's just leave it at that."

"Okay, so I guess talking about others in our lives is something we can't do anymore. We used to."

"We used to do a lot of things, but what purpose does it serve to talk about it now? We'd be better off just getting through the rest of this. I don't need to know the details." Pride made him say the next words, but he refused to listen to her explanation of a life he wouldn't be in. "I'm happy, Morgan, I'm glad you will be too."

There it was, he was pushing her away, he'd found someone else. She heard the anger in his voice, in Morgan's mind she thought maybe he'd been homesick for his girlfriend, maybe he was getting anxious now to get back home and resume the life he'd built without her, Morgan didn't mention anything else.

As she lay alone that night in her bed, she tossed and turned as she normally did. But it wasn't the nightmare that haunted her thoughts, it was her restlessness where Ryder was concerned, the question of whether they still had something to salvage. But he said he was happy, did she have a right to think she could just step back into his life where she'd once stepped out?

As if her place had been saved in line and she could just take up where they'd left off. In the back of her mind, she harbored that's how it would be. He was waiting for her, he would always be there, would always love her. How could he not always love her?

CHAPTER FOURTEEN

Ketchikan, the fourth largest town in Alaska, is touted as home to some of the most beautiful native culture in the world. Legend, which abounds in Alaska, had it that the word Ketchikan originated from the Tlingit word 'Kitcxam', which means 'Where the eagles' wings are.' All one had to do was look to the trees and see what would appear to be golf balls, when in actuality it was eagles perched high in majestic beauty.

Deeply rooted in native culture it boasted the largest totem collection in the world and offered dance, craft demonstrations and artifact exhibits to show tourists a little of their way of life. Named one of the top 100 Small Arts Communities in the United States, one could learn more from museums like Tongass historical museum and Dolly's House, the parks and cultural centers like Saxman, Totem Bight and Totem Heritage Center or one could walk through town along Historic Creek Street on a wooden boardwalk that winds along the shores of Ketchikan Creek to get a taste of their way of life.

Known as the 'Salmon Capital of the World', fishing visitors tested their skills for an impressive variety of salmon, halibut and other bottom dwellers along with fresh water trout and steelhead. Partake in boating activities that were easily accessed, or take a breathtaking excursion through the wilderness surrounding Ketchikan to Misty Fjords National monument that was accessible by air or boat.

Another thing Ketchikan offered that was unique, the community of Metlakatla on Annette Island nearby, the only Indian reservation in the state of Alaska. Ketchikan along with its neighboring communities provided an unforgettable Alaska experience along the Inside Passage.

****

That morning over breakfast Jerry was excited at another day before them. "Another day we've been blessed with and shouldn't let it go to waste. You coming with me today to wrangle up some fun?" He asked Bea then directed his question to all. "What say all of us find ourselves a bear to ride or something?"

Bea laughed. "They don't ride bears. Do they?"

Ryder had to laugh at the question in her voice, her worry it could possibly be so. "I don't think it's a sport, but I wouldn't put anything past Jerry."

"What about you two? What do you have planned for the day?" Jerry asked both Ryder and Morgan.

Morgan shrugged. "I was kind of looking forward to bear riding."

Ryder laughed. "You almost knocked over the kayak the other day when you thought one was coming after us."

Morgan countered quickly. "This is a brand new day, isn't it?"

"What are your plans, Ryder?" Jerry asked.

"Fishing, anyone care to join me?"

"Not me." Bea immediately answered. "I never did fish."

"Neither did I, but as I said, it's a brand new day." Morgan finished her coffee and directed her words to Ryder. "Interested in me tagging along?"

"You've been tagging along behind me since you learned to walk, can I stop you now?"

"Tagging along? There were many times you were the one on my heels."

"That was only because you'd stolen my baseball and wouldn't give it back."

"Baseball, baseball. It was always about baseball."

Not always, Ryder thought to himself, but didn't say the words, there was no point in them. Bea and Jerry smiled between them as Ryder and Morgan joked and bantered back and forth for several minutes. Ryder was surprised, but she did join him for fishing. He enjoyed the transformation taking place for however long it would last, enjoyed seeing a genuine smile on her face, the true laughter as it rang out when she reeled in a fish and fell in her attempt.

"Now I have a true story of the one that got away." Morgan took his hand when he offered to help her up. "I never thought I'd be in the wilds of Alaska fishing with you, but at least I have a witness. He was huge, wasn't he? Can I use it as a big fish tale of my own? The big one that got away?"

"Your father would be proud you'd have a fish story to tell. It was probably the only thing you never did with him, go fishing."

"He always had you for that." She wiped her hands. "I never liked the stink of it, and couldn't stomach the gutting part."

"And you still grew up to be a doctor."

"Delivering babies, certainly not gutting people."

Ryder looked to her, his voice softer. "He'd be proud of you. You're a good doctor, Morgan, and not a half bad fisherman."

"Fisherwoman. Is there such a word? And why do you think he'd have been surprised I'm a good doctor? And how do you know I'm a good doctor anyway, are you just saying that because you're guessing?"

"I've run into a few people over the years. Your name's come up."

"The latest being Evan and Ray." She wanted to bring the subject up again, wanted to talk about it and explain to see if it would make a difference.

"They speak very highly of you."

"They're friends, they have to," she teased.

"No they don't."

"Ryder, I…" Morgan hesitated and touched his arm.

"Don't explain him, don't feel like you have to make apologies for having a life, I never expected you to live the rest of your life alone. I told you, I have someone else and you have someone else. We're happy with other people let's just leave it at that."

It bothered her but she didn't say anything else about it when he was so insistent she shouldn't. "You're spoken very highly of also. I never expected less from you, I knew what kind of doctor you'd be since the time you saved that squirrel all on your own."

"You helped. Think that was the beginning of our careers? Taking care of a wounded animal?" He remembered what she spoke of, remembered her help as they nurtured it night and day back to life. When they set it free it often showed up on either of their windowsills as if to say a quick hello, and to give thanks.

"Wonder what ever happened to that little guy and his family. I know he must have had generations that are probably still running all over the yard."

"I'm sure they are. Some things bury their roots and can't leave."

She heard the insinuation in his voice but didn't want to argue, didn't want to ruin the good mood between them. "What are the new owners like? Have you met them?"

It was the first time she questioned the people who'd purchased the house, the first time she'd had a desire to. Only now did she think it had been a mistake and she should have asked her mother to hold on to it a little longer.

"My parents think their new neighbor is the next best thing to sliced bread."

"Someone from the city?"

"Yeah," he answered honestly.

"So guess it all worked out." She said with a distant tone. It was too late to do anything about it now and she regretted her decision made in haste.

Now that she could see a fog lifting, she could see the mistake she'd made. She should have given herself more time, her mother was willing to hold onto the house until she'd be ready, but maybe it was for the best. She just wished now she had the chance to go back for one last time.

Morgan sat back and watched him fish. His muscular body so familiar, a wanting and yearning she hadn't felt in her numbness over the years began to emerge and now she'd have to learn to push that aside. He'd always had the ability to make her need to touch him, she felt so connected when she did, but he stood in the distance now and she reached out with words instead.

Morgan became quiet, watched as Ryder cast out his line again, as he tried to hide still, his hurt. "I'm sorry, Ryder."

"Sorry? For what?"

"For leaving you, for calling you on the phone to break up our relationship, but I couldn't face you, I couldn't go back there."

He didn't say anything as he thought about what she'd said. She'd never apologized for doing what she did, and he took her words to heart, appreciated hearing them.

"All behind us."

"Yeah," she whispered.

It was sad they'd shared so much of a lifetime and that's all there was to say about it now. That it was all behind them.

"I'm sorry too, Morgan," Ryder said after a few quiet moments.

"For?"

"That I couldn't save them for you."

"They were already dead when we got to the hospital, there wasn't anything you could do."

"I would have done that for you if I could have."

Morgan stepped closer to him and touched his arm, she needed to feel him. "I know you would have, you loved them too."

He would have sold his soul to the devil to avoid that night in their lives. He'd been there at the hospital when they'd brought them in, was there in the very beginning of Morgan's own death, the emotional death she suffered and he could still hear her shrill cries of torturous pain in his own nightmares he suffered. Ryder could still feel her in his arms as he held her back from going after them when they rolled the cart of their covered dead bodies through the door and she never saw them again.

And he too lost some of the most important people in his life. Like her, Ryder suffered through it also. At times, still did. Not to the same degree, but he had no one to ease his pain. At least now she acknowledged she wasn't the only one to bear the burden of death.

Morgan stepped so close to him, reached up and touched his face tenderly with compassion, a love she still felt. "I'm sorry I wasn't there for you. I was selfish to think I was the only one, I know that."

Ryder couldn't stop himself, he placed his lips tenderly to hers, the softness of them, his longing for her, made him lose all sense and he reached around and took her in his arms. A tender spontaneous kiss he gave no second thought to. Morgan responded by melting into him, her body pressed to his, her hand came up and held his face to hers.

Just as suddenly as he'd kissed her, Ryder pulled away, could slap himself for his moment of weakness, a moment that wouldn't help him along the next few days until she was gone again. "I won't do this, Morgan."

"It was a kiss, it wasn't wrong."

"I won't be pulled back in, and I won't be a replacement because Evan isn't here for you right now and you need to be close to someone."

Morgan felt hurt by his accusation. "You know that isn't true."

"Isn't it?"

"We're friends, we always have been."

"No we're not. We moved past friends a long time ago when we moved from the front seat to the back seat of an old car. There's too much between us now and we can't go back to being nothing more than innocent friends."

She didn't like that he pulled away from her. "Think Stella wouldn't approve?"

"She'd approve as much as Evan would. Maybe we should stay away from each other for the rest of the week. I don't like being a replacement because you don't have who you really want."

"You were the one who kissed me, and that wasn't what happened anyway."

"Isn't it? Did it mean anything other than the fact that you needed to feel close to someone? Anyone? Guess you should be glad it was me standing here and not some stranger."

He felt it was what she'd done, simply needed to feel close to someone in that split second and it wouldn't have mattered who was in front of her.

She stood quiet for a long time. Morgan wasn't sure how to answer his question, tell him the truth that she loved him and always would? Tell him there was nowhere else on earth she'd rather be than wrapped in his arms? Wrapped in his life? But his anger stopped her, she saw it as him feeling guilty he'd been unfaithful to Stella with the kiss, now he regretted it.

"Just because you're angry with yourself for kissing someone else, doesn't mean you have to be angry with me." She was angry now too, they seemed to do that to each other.

"What reason do I have to be mad at you? You walked out on me with nothing but a phone call six months later to tell me it was over, to tell me to get on with my life."

"And you did, so what's the point in arguing about it now?" She lashed out.

Ryder debated his next words and decided to tell her what he'd done. He didn't care about his pride that suffered on that day, didn't care how it would make him look, he wanted her to know that he hadn't given up without a last futile attempt at hope. "I showed up on our wedding day. No one else in town did, Bea told everyone the wedding was called off but I was there, all dressed in my tux. It was just the minister and I, he finally left and I waited for so long, for some reason I thought all you needed was time away, that you'd never forget our wedding day and that would be the day you'd come back to me," he paused then continued, his voice just slightly calmer. "I was there, I waited, and you never came. Mad? No, I'm not mad anymore. I'm far from feeling anything anymore. If nothing, I'm certainly smarter now than to be pulled in by you so you can toss me aside again."

"I know I hurt you, and I'm..."

Ryder wouldn't let her finish. "And you're sorry, you've said that. I thought it would mean so much more by now but I'm not even sure what to make of those words. What do you want? Do you want a relationship? You want to go back to where we were?"

"I'm not saying I want anything."

"That's the point." Ryder commented and roughly pulled his fishing line in. It was time to go back, he would do as he said and try to stay away from her for the rest of their time.

Morgan was confused. Just when she thought she was getting her emotions in order, more emotions overwhelmed her. What were her plans? She'd been going in one direction, it wasn't easy to just decide on the spur of the moment that she wanted her life back, and it wasn't fair to Ryder. She still had things to work through, still had to fully heal. Was that what she wanted now? Her entire life back again?

He had a life with someone, Stella waited for him at home. Was it fair for her to disrupt their lives on a whim? And did he love her still? Or were his emotions a jealousy over Evan? He hadn't the benefit of knowing what she did, that Evan meant nothing to her.

Dinner that evening was subdued, the tension between Ryder and Morgan was so noticeable one could almost reach out and touch it. They all got through it, and afterwards, Jerry approached her.

"You realize you're not the only one who has to heal? Ryder's been suffering a long time too."

"Ryder hates me, as well he should."

"He thinks you have someone else in your life and it hurts him. Yeah," Jerry said with a small chuckle of humor. "He hates you right now."

"You don't have to agree so easily."

"Why do you want him to hate you? Why won't you tell him the truth?"

Morgan looked at him oddly, how could he know so much? "How do you know it isn't the truth? How do you know I don't have someone else?"

"I pay attention to life now, more than I ever did before. I found I have a knack for knowing things." He went back to his question. "So why don't you tell him the truth?"

"He's got someone, why shouldn't I?"

"After all this time you're going to let pride stand in your way? Each of you jealous the other has a life, even if it isn't the life either of you want?" Jerry laughed. "How complicated we make things. If going through this world were easy, it wouldn't be so darn entertaining and funny."

"He's getting married to her so it must be the life he wants. I don't even know why he had to come."

"Why do you think?"

"Because he loved Daddy, it's only out of respect for him that he's here."

"Maybe, but maybe for other reasons. Are you going to let it die right here, Morgan? Are you going to let yourself suffer another death?"

"He's the one that gave up already."

"Already? He's waited an awfully long time."

"And then he gave up," she said it accusingly, angry he had.

"Hmph." Jerry huffed.

"What's that supposed to mean?"

"I'm not puttin' my nose into this one, you two have to battle it out for yourselves." He laughed and shook his head. "It will either be on the battlefield or in the bedroom, but you two will have at it."

She looked over to Ryder who was standing at the bar with a few of Bea and Jerry's friends. He was smoking a cigar and talking to a few of the men, looked so out of place in age, yet looked right at home among them. She could tell from the loud boisterous laughter among the group, and the empty glasses in front of them, their shots of whiskey were taking their toll.

The waitress flirted outrageously with him and Morgan turned away. "There's nothing to get into anyway, Ryder will be fine. He is fine."

"Ryder's a proud man. He's a good man. I know Bea and your father couldn't have asked for a better man for their daughter."

"And as I said, out of respect for my father is the only reason he's here."

"Don't you see it as one of those neon signs? Can't you see the meaning of it?" Jerry shook his head at her inattention. "Like a big ole' grizzly coming straight for you and you don't take notice. Shoo it away like a little fly on shit."

"Well I guess they never counted on him falling in love with someone else, did they?"

"Ryder is a man in love alright, if he wasn't, he wouldn't be here."

Jerry left her then, left her more confused than ever. Why was she paying attention to him? Why did she put any credence to anything Jerry said? He talked about flies on shit.

She eventually moved closer to the crowd of people, found herself jostled around a bit and when she was next to Ryder, he didn't say a word, just took her arm and led her to the dance floor.

"You're enjoying yourself this evening." She laughed as he spun her first before he pulled her close.

"Why not? A few more days and I'll be able to go home." He thought the whiskey would help with getting Morgan off his mind but that was impossible, whiskey would never help, nothing would. "Just a few more days, I need to get home."

"Wedding plans to tend to I imagine." She said the words before she thought about them. It's what had been on her mind. "Will I at least be invited?"

"No," he stated with ease.

"Good, I didn't want to have to shop for a gift."

"You'd probably get me something stupid anyway, like a case of peanut butter."

"I'd splurge and get the jelly to go with it. Is it still strawberry?"

"And I guess like me knowing you, you know me better than anyone else on earth."

"Hard not to." She thought about the other morning when he'd helped her through the night. She'd noticed the sliding glass door wasn't open. "But maybe you've changed. You used to sleep with the window open, the other morning when you were in my room, it wasn't open."

He looked at her for a moment before he spoke. "You never noticed when we were older and you stayed at my apartment in the city, that the window wasn't open?"

She thought about it and it took her a moment to realize it hadn't been. "I never noticed then, I didn't pay attention to it anyway. But you'd always sleep with it open at your mother's house, always, even in the dead of winter with snow on the ground."

"My window was only always open, for you to come inside."

Morgan would sneak out of her house at times and go to his. Climb to the roof of the garage then slip easily inside his window. They were young and it wasn't for anything more than his companionship as they'd talk all night long. There were many things she remembered about Ryder, spent years as a young child playing with him, while May, always more interested in playing girly games, wouldn't play with her. Morgan always interested in tomboyish things. Somewhere along the way, she and Ryder had fallen in love.

When it happened, she was never really sure. How it happened, she was never really sure. But somewhere between fighting over the same pool toy when they were three, to planning their wedding day, they'd discovered life would never be the same without the other. As Morgan thought of it now, looked into eyes she used to know so well, she wondered when Ryder discovered otherwise. He didn't sleep with his window open anymore.

Ryder stared at her for a long time, his broad smile faded now and he held her so close to him. "I can't go back there again, Morgan. I can't go through what I did, so I have no hopes for us now. It's better that way."

"Yeah, it's better that way." She reluctantly agreed quietly. It was his apology for not loving her anymore, his excuse and explanation instead of coming out and telling her he'd fallen in love with someone else.

That night, neither slept as they lay lost in their misgivings on the other's lives. Each envisioned what the others lives were like, and each was wrong in their assumptions but they didn't know that. And in solitary pain over everything they'd lost, they lay alone.

CHAPTER FIFTEEN

Located on the southern tip of Vancouver Island, Victoria was the largest of British Columbia's 6,500 islands. It boasted the mildest climate Canada had to offer and gave residents and tourists a place of sunshine and calm serenity as it was surrounded by water and peaceful untouched land.

World class attractions delighted visitors and pulled them to Vancouver Island where the sky seemed bluer, the air clearer and out of the mist and haze of an Alaska chill, came a glorious day of sunshine. One could immerse themselves in the culture of the city among beautiful historic buildings, and look up to see the serenity of snowcapped mountain peaks. It was a diverse city that offered much to be explored.

As the ship sailed towards their final port destination, the day was filled with activities or solitude, whatever one chose. Morgan took yet another chance to wrap herself in a solitary world where she was finding contentment within, took quiet moments to let the comfort she was finally discovering sink in. As she said goodbye to Alaska, she let a peace fill her. A peace she could carry with her and expand on, one she finally allowed herself to let in. And as she said goodbye to Alaska, she felt she was finally saying goodbye to her father and May, something she'd never been able to do, something she desperately needed to do.

There were many things that had stopped her before, but now she allowed herself to let go, to set them free. She envisioned them among the spirits of the northern lights, closed her eyes and wished them a safe journey to heaven, and she apologized silently that it had taken her so long. She even imagined May's sigh and what she would say.

"It's about time, Morgan, you always had to hold onto everything much longer than you needed to."

Morgan suspected it was their odd intuition together that she missed the most, someone who knew what to say or do, someone who understood without words. A connection and tie that was unbearably painful to break, but it was necessary for survival. May knew it, and Morgan discovered it, for it was only her that selfishly held on.

She could have used those thoughts to describe both May and Ryder. The difference was that Ryder still walked the earth, and maybe breaking ties to him was necessary for survival also. Maybe that's what May wanted her to see, that she held onto him but it was time to let go now. Had both her and her father wanted Morgan to see his life with someone else? Push her along on the way elsewhere?

She pushed that passing thought aside for another time and Morgan grieved their deaths. Something she hadn't fully allowed herself to do before, but slowly she let go of her blame, was consoled and reassured their deaths were no fault of her own, they were just as May tried to tell her, Gods will. The message was only now beginning to be accepted and understood. Everyone had recovered and moved forward, it was now time for Morgan to discover what lay in the aftermath of their deaths. She would have to release the past and discover life again, it's what they wanted from her and she knew that as she looked out to a cloudless blue sky.

"There you are, I haven't seen you all day and I was beginning to worry about you." Bea stepped next to her along the top deck of the ship. Her apprehension eased when Morgan turned to her and smiled.

"No need to worry."

She touched her daughters face with a tenderness, tears came to her eyes. "I see that. You're really going to be okay now, aren't you?"

"I'm going to be okay, Mama," she stated with a conviction, there was no hesitation in her words.

"I can't tell you how happy that makes me, I've worried about you so. One of these days when you have a child of your own, you'll know the helpless pain a mother feels when her child is hurting."

"I'm sorry I wouldn't let you in. I'm sorry I wouldn't let you help." She paused and chuckled. "It seems all I've been doing lately is apologizing. To you, to Ryder."

"You and Ryder getting along? I can't tell, one minute I think you are, and the next it doesn't seem that way."

"As well as we can I guess. I think we're both looking forward to being apart."

"There was a time you couldn't stand to be apart. I remember watching him climb over the fence as soon as he could walk and toddle over to the house for breakfast, always wanted cheese toast. I think he still calls it yellow toast to this day." Bea laughed, could picture the little boy in her mind, even though he was a handsome grown man now.

"Mom, not everything is going to be the same. I may be dealing with my grief now, slowly, I feel like I am, but that doesn't mean things will be the same."

"Nothing stays the same, does it?" Bea sighed. "So many things aren't what I expected them to be. We think life is one way and we're surprised to find ourselves somewhere different."

"You accepted it a lot sooner than I did. I don't fault you for embracing it, had I done the same..." Morgan thought of what could have been had she embraced the change sooner and not lost Ryder. "I don't know what's to become of you and Jerry, but I'm sorry I didn't give him a chance in the beginning, I'm sorry I judged him. That wasn't like me, but I haven't been myself. It's the only excuse I have." Morgan laughed. "There I go again, apologizing for something else. Maybe I should wear a big sign across my chest to save me the trouble."

"I never thought I'd ever love a man again, but I can see myself loving Jerry."

"I found out it's been much longer than I thought, I was waiting for you to tell me. Why didn't you tell me sooner?"

"We talked very little."

"I should have been there for you." Morgan said honestly.

"You couldn't be, you couldn't even be there for yourself. I understand Morgan, I understand why you couldn't be there, but I made my way. And I learned I could make my way."

Morgan looked over to Jerry and Ryder who were walking towards them, ready for dinner. They were going to go into Victoria to a restaurant Jerry knew of. Morgan smiled with a sadness.

"I guess I'll have to learn that now too."

Bea looked to the two who approached. "An odd picture we make. I never would have thought a month ago I'd be on a ship in Victoria British Columbia with you, Ryder, and an overgrown cowboy who wears the loudest clothes I've ever seen." Bea laughed. "I'm going to work on toning that down."

She looked to her mother. "So you plan on being with him for awhile?"

"If he'll have me." Bea took her daughters hand. "It doesn't mean I love your father any less. There will never be another man to take his place."

She knew exactly what she spoke of. It was the same with Ryder, there would never be another to take his place. But hopefully, one day, she wouldn't be opposed to finding someone to share her life with. Maybe there would be someone out there for her, but it would never be the same. Yet another thing she would have to accept and overcome.

"The two most beautiful women in the world, and I feel it an honor to be able to spend an evening with them." Jerry said when he reached them. "You two are prettier than a plump pig with an apple in his mouth."

Morgan burst into laughter. "You put that so eloquently, I'm not quite sure it's a compliment, but I'll take it as such."

He was so opposite what her father had been. Henry Bailey was a quiet, subdued man and this man before her something entirely different, but Morgan quickly stopped herself from the comparison, there was no comparison to be made. As different as they were, she could picture her father laughing in his approval of Bea's choice. Jerry would offer her a different way of life for the next leg of her lifetime journey. And when it was over, he would be waiting for her to hear all about it.

Morgan was relaxed that evening, the most relaxed she'd been in a very long time. The restaurant Jerry took them to was lovely and quaint as they sat on a deck overlooking the bay with snow capped mountains in the distance. It was odd to see the snow and yet they were ensconced in a warm summer breeze. They were serenaded by music and Jerry led Bea onto the dance floor to a slow romantic song.

"Shall we?" Ryder asked as he rose from the table and indicated the dance floor.

"Why should they have all the fun?"

He pulled her easily into his arms, she fit well, always had. "I haven't even mentioned how good you look tonight, you look amazing."

Morgan was wearing the much too short dress Emily and Amy made her purchase when she spent the weekend with them. She'd grabbed it at the last minute when she realized she didn't have much to choose from in her closet.

"Well thank you. It wasn't something I picked out, but it's better than my doctor's whites. I let a very modern young teen talk me into it."

"If I knew her, I'd thank her. Me and the dozen other men that have been eying you since we walked in."

Morgan blushed. "You're only trying to flatter me, what do you want?"

Ryder didn't tell her what he truly wanted, he couldn't. Morgan needed to figure that out on her own without being forced or pressured. Was it him? Was it Evan? Ryder was unsure and it had to come from Morgan, and she'd indicated nothing.

Jerry came up to them and interrupted, wanted to cut in so Ryder danced with Bea and they both laughed as Jerry literally swept Morgan off her feet as he picked her up and twirled her around. She protested immediately but her laughter rang out.

"I love that sound." Bea said with a smile as she looked to her daughter.

"I've missed it too."

"If we'd have known Alaska would do it, we could have brought her years ago. Was it Alaska?"

"I'm not sure what it was, but I'm grateful for it." Ryder smiled as he watched the two. "Hardly a trip we'll forget anytime soon."

"People don't forget things, I think she needs more time, but she'll…"

Ryder interrupted when he knew what she was going to say. "I can't live on false hope, Bea, I've done it too long now. Nothings changed between Morgan and I, all I want is closure."

"I couldn't help but hope. You two just... well, two people who can communicate with a flashlight certainly have a bond."

Ryder laughed. "I never understood a word she said, I just pretended I did."

"She probably didn't either, and she just pretended too. But you still communicated something back and forth in the middle of the night. I remember getting up for water sometimes and seeing you from the kitchen window."

"A long time ago, Bea, a long time ago." He looked to Morgan who smiled and laughed as Jerry twirled her around with an expert skill. "I guess we're all ready to live the second half of our lives. I wish someone would have told me I'd have two, I always thought it was one."

"And if you'd have known?"

Ryder thought about her question before he answered with sadness in his tone. "I certainly can't have any regrets, I'll never regret Morgan. I wouldn't have missed any of it."

When the song ended, Bea went back to dancing with Jerry and Ryder and Morgan sat back down. Morgan watched the two as her sentimental heart swelled. Happiness for her mother was all she could wish, and she could see she had achieved it.

Ryder smiled at the acceptance he saw in her eyes. "Who would have thought?"

"Indeed. A strange picture they make, but yet it makes sense, I don't know why."

He was glad something made sense to her. He was finding sense of very little, and it had nothing to do with Jerry and Bea. "I suppose I should start getting used to Bea not being around Beach Lake. I have a feeling I'll never get used to the idea, but left with no choice, guess I'll have to. I'll miss her."

"Her condo isn't too far away, I'm sure she'll visit often."

"I wasn't talking about her condo, I was talking about her moving to Texas. I have a feeling she'll be there soon, probably even riding that bull Jerry talked about."

"You think?" It was a notion Morgan hadn't thought about, but she supposed he was right.

"Does that worry you?"

Morgan hesitated. "I never really thought about it. It isn't her moving to Texas that worries me, it... it seems odd that I'll never have a reason to return to Beach Lake."

Ryder could be her reason, but she didn't even entertain the notion. It didn't upset him on the outside, he was trying to come to terms with it and pushed his thoughts aside so as not to get angry. "It's hard letting go of something that's been your life for so long." His words indicated much more that what they talked of.

Morgan heard his hidden meaning and sighed. "Change is so hard to get through, so many things have changed over the years and I wasn't even aware of it. Look at Mama, she's such a different person and I don't even know when that happened, and you..." she paused before she went on. "You've done so well for yourself, of course it isn't anything I wouldn't have expected. Everyone has been living, and I've just been stuck somewhere."

Ryder thought of the life she had that she didn't talk about, she gave him the feeling that she somehow wanted to hold onto both, her old and new life. But Morgan had choices to make, one or the other, and those choices had to come from her heart or he would forever wonder about it. She had to let go of something, and her not talking about their relationship indicated it was him she had to let go of.

He couldn't wait on Morgan, he'd done that for years now and he had to somehow move past it. He'd go home and marry Stella, it's what she wanted, and why shouldn't he at least have someone to share his life with. Even if he could never give her all he'd given Morgan, as she said herself, things changed and one had to adjust.

Morgan looked out to the captivating scenery she would remember for a long time. "I don't want this day to be over. It's going much too soon and I don't want it to end."

"I have no control over that."

"Can't you do something to stop it?"

"Not my area of expertise, I wouldn't know where to begin."

She took his hand in hers. "I want the day to stop, Ryder. I'm not ready, I have a feeling I'll never see you again after tomorrow."

"There'd be no reason to."

She wanted him, she loved him, and as much as she wanted to say the words she couldn't. She was being selfish, just as she had been the last few years, to think he should stop his life for her. "Ryder, I..." The words of love were almost out and yet she stopped herself. He didn't need his life complicated by the knowledge she still loved him. Would it complicate it? Would it make a difference to him? But she couldn't get the words out. "I'm glad we've had this time together."

"I'm glad I came. It's helped me to see things more clearly, put some closure on something I needed closure on. Maybe both of us were sent here to do that, I've always thought everything was left undone, maybe this was meant to be our official end to our lives together."

It hit her then. That was the reason her father and May probably wanted the two together, to put closure on it, not to reunite, but to put closure and tell her to move past it. Okay, so she could see the signs, she could take meaning from them, but she didn't like it. Morgan had a sad expression and Ryder touched her face.

"Maybe," she said quietly. "That doesn't mean I have to like it."

"You'll be okay now, I really believe that, and I'm glad I know. I've spent a lot of time worrying about you, at least now I know I won't have to anymore."

"What about you, Ryder? Are you going to be okay? Are you going to have a good life?"

"It's shaping up, I'll get through it."

"It's more than getting through it, I'd like to think you're happy, I picture you in a big old house with tons of kids, coaching the baseball team and at the same time going to ballet recitals for a little girl who loves her daddy. You'll be a good father someday, you've always reminded me of my own. Kind, honest, a man who doesn't compromise his morals and values, you're a rare breed in this day and age Ryder, and Stella is very lucky. I hope she knows that."

Morgan had lost him, but she would learn to be happy for him. It came out of the unconditional love she had for Ryder and always would. It was sad that was all they had left with. After a lifetime together, they could only talk about the life they wouldn't have. A life filled with other people and other dreams. At a different time, a different place, they'd talked about different things, but not now.

That night, Morgan slipped into Ryder's room and quietly slipped into his bed. As he took her in his arms they were each driven by a need, one of desperation to take what they could before they'd have to give it up. They came together silently, no words spoken as a familiar passion consumed them, a passion that was never far from their minds, and it filled their senses with everything they would let go of.

With each second that passed and as the ship sailed closer and closer to home port, they felt an urgent need to take what they could as it slipped further and further behind them. Take what they could until they'd have to leave it all behind for the final time.

Both needed one last time together to carry them through the long nights that lay ahead, empty nights of loneliness that would need to be filled. They would take with them that morning, the memory of their emotion filled union, sad consolation compared to the lifetime they once expected from one another.

It was poignant and heartbreaking to know it would be the last time they'd ever see each other again. But Morgan coveted close the sweet memory to carry with her when she left, and when Ryder woke to his empty bed, he too coveted close the sweet memory to sustain him. He whispered to the silent room.

"Goodbye, Morgan."

CHAPTER SIXTEEN

"Well little filly, did you find what you came to find?" He could see it in her eyes but Jerry asked anyway, wanted to hear the admission.

They were standing on the quiet deck as the ship pulled back into its home berth in Seattle and Morgan thought about the question. She looked for signs of her father, signs of her sister. Had she found them? There was nothing substantial, nothing she could physically prove or tangible that she could hold in her hands, but regardless, she found something. Question was, had it all been in her mind? Morgan stood with a perplexed look, didn't answer his question as Jerry spoke again.

"You found what they wanted you to find." Jerry squeezed her hand tight. "I have a feeling you'll start living again Morgan. We're only put here for a short time, and if your time isn't going to be done till years from now, you have nothing to say about it. And that could be a very long time to die the slow death you were dying."

She felt like she were dying that slow death again as she could still feel Ryder's gentle touch, and yet in just a short time she would have to watch him leave her, go back to the woman he loved and that wasn't her anymore, back to a life she was no longer a part of. "Life will never be easy, will it?"

"If it were easy, we'd have no character. Obstacles we overcome only make us stronger, makes us into the people we are. They're put in our way to teach us something, it's up to us to figure out what."

"I never would have thought you a great philosopher, but you seem to have a good grasp on life."

"Forced upon me. After losing my family, I was looking for answers too. Through all the pain, I found the peace I needed to find. I had to, for my grandson and for me."

"The legend of the northern lights, the spirits of the dead on their way to heaven, is that legend real? Or did you make it up?"

"What do you think?"

Morgan wasn't sure what she thought, she'd like to believe it were so. "I think you would have said anything to try and make me like you."

"Maybe," he smiled mischievously. "But you should know by now, I don't say things for the benefit of others. I say what I feel."

"Regardless, whether it's true or not, thank you for sharing it with me."

"Don't thank me, I wasn't the one who lead you there."

"No," she stated softly. "I guess you weren't."

Morgan watched as he walked away, watched as her mother looked up from talking and the smile that spread across her face was instant. In that moment, she knew what she'd found. She found life again. She found the simple pleasure of watching an eagle in flight. She discovered she was but a small miniscule piece in the grand scheme of things. The world would go on without her, it had before and would continue to do so until she decided to fully join the living again.

She also found an odd sense of peace from an old garish cowboy who'd taught her things she never expected to learn. Was it him? The words he'd said? Was it the atmosphere of Alaska? It could have been a number of things and she would never know for sure exactly what. What she did know, was that it was her father and May who'd sent her there. She'd carried a heavy burden with her, but would leave it behind and not carry it any longer when the ship returned to its home port. Morgan knew that for sure as she watched in the distance a bird that soared towards the heavens above. Was it an eagle? Proud in its glory?

"Morgan?" Ryder asked from beside her. He'd called to her three times and she hadn't heard, she looked up now with a start.

"Yeah? Oh, Ryder, I..." She paused as she was brought down from her thoughts. "I'm sorry, I didn't hear you. Did you say something?"

"Have a safe trip back to Minneapolis."

"You're leaving?" She said in a panic at his words.

"I have a very early flight, so I'm getting off in a few minutes."

"I just thought..." She paused. What did she think?

Ryder waited patiently, but when she spoke again it wasn't what he wanted to hear. He wanted to hear she'd had a change of heart, had come to realize she'd always loved him and always would.

Morgan continued. "I just thought maybe we'd have time for coffee or something."

"I guess we don't."

He didn't want to sit and have coffee, prolong it any more than it needed to be. She'd given herself to him so freely the night before as she lay in his arms, yet she hadn't changed her mind. Morgan was possibly on her way back to life, but she wasn't on her way back to him, Ryder had to accept that and wish her well.

She stared at him for a long time. The familiar face she envisioned in her dreams, the face she'd seen every day of her life for so many years. She could still feel his skin on hers, the feel of his nearness. How did one put an end to that? How did one say goodbye to someone so important? The direction of her life was still unknown, and he seemed to have his all planned out.

Did she take the chance? Blurt it out they were making a mistake and belonged together? She had no right to tear apart his life again, he was happy, he'd told her so. And he'd closed that window long ago.

She said the natural thing friends would say. "If you're ever in..."

But Ryder stopped her invitation to visit if he were ever in the town she lived. He didn't need to hear words mere acquaintances would say to one another. "I won't be."

"I never thought it would be this way. I never thought the last time I would ever see you again would be like this."

Ryder touched her face tenderly, the words he spoke were from a long ago childhood and when they were in love. "Sweet dreams, Morgan."

When they sat in the back yard or on the front porch till all hours of the night, whenever he left, he'd say the words just before jumping over the fence to his house. When he was on the other side, out of eyeshot, he always added, 'until tomorrow'. She'd heard his voice in the middle of the night at times, it's what helped her through the lonely years, she'd taken for granted there would always be a tomorrow for them, was sure their connection could never be broken.

She placed her hand over his and held it to her cheek. He didn't add the words now, didn't say 'until tomorrow'. After sharing their lives, all she could do was watch him leave. There was so much she needed to say, so much she needed from him, now felt even emptier. Had he turned around, he would have seen the tears that came as she stood in her isolated sorrow at the loss of so many things.

Morgan stood for a long time as people milled about. Tons of people with faces she couldn't see walked around her, all she could see was Ryder leaving her. Just when she thought she was on the verge of living, why did it seem the world crashed down around her again? She'd done it to herself. She'd wanted to be alone, pushed him out and she'd lost him for good now. She should be happy for him and the future he would have, but all she kept thinking about was herself and how foolish she'd been to let him slip away.

Some things you didn't realize until it was too late. In the quiet of her mind, she wished he and Stella well.

****

When Morgan settled back into her life in Minneapolis it seemed all her patients waited for her to return. Babies that should have been born while she was gone hadn't been, they had all waited for her instead. Babies that should have been born later, decided to come early and because of it all she spent two weeks on a non-stop schedule of deliveries.

She wasn't surprised when her mother called and told her of plans to go to Texas.

"Come out and visit as soon as you can, I'll be there for a month." Bea said and tried to encourage her. "I'm trying with Jerry, but he's talking about matching outfits."

Morgan laughed. "Please, Mama, please don't let it happen, I can't see you in sequins."

"I won't be, but I may need your help. He listened to you about the steaks, doesn't eat so much red meat now, he likes my chicken."

"I'll try to come sometime." When she hung up the phone Morgan smiled at the vision of her mother on a bull wearing a red sequined outfit and a humongous cowboy hat.

One of the partners came into her office and saw her there with that huge smile.

"Good news?" He asked at the look on her face.

"My mother, she's moving to Texas," then she laughed. "It's too much to explain."

"Just wanted to give you these files you wanted." He set them down on the desk. "New patients while you were away."

She looked to the top folder and the name on it didn't cause her pain, instead she laughed. "Who names their child Henry? In this modern age, who names their child Henry?"

She was more settled about it now, before, she probably would have broken down and cried, but she'd laughed instead. A little 'hello' from her father? A little 'goodbye'? Morgan shook her head and laughed again.

She hadn't had time for anything but a quick phone call to tell Nancy she was home and back to being busy with work, and out of the obligation of friendship, she knew she should call Evan and kept meaning to, but they ran into each other at the hospital before she could.

They literally ran into each other as Morgan was dashing in and he was dashing out. She bumped into him and he grabbed her to keep her from falling.

"I'm sorry, I..." Then he realized it was her and laughed. "Morgan."

"Hey stranger, I've been meaning to call you."

"That's what they all say," he teased with a broad smile.

"I have a mother whose ten centimeters dilated right now, you going to be in town long? Meet me for dinner later?"

"Call me when you're through." He dashed off in his direction and she in hers.

Her patient had complications and it had taken much longer than planned, so they met up late that night. The only thing that was open was the greasy hamburger joint around the corner and they sat in a booth with the years of wear that showed on the old vinyl seats.

"I knew you must have been back, I even gave you a phone and I still get no call," he teased.

"I'll take punishment of thirty lashes, my gallant sir, but I've been playing catch up. All the babies waited for me."

He had waited also, anxious to see her but didn't want to push so he hadn't called her. "I was beginning to worry about you, but I see there was no need, you look great, Morgan. That vacation did you a world of good."

He saw an immediate difference in her, she actually looked relaxed and a little content, looked like a very different woman than the one he sat with on the kitchen floor the eve of her departure. The one filled with nervous apprehension and unease.

"Alaska was beautiful, I never imagined what a little clean air and Angel mist could do for a soul."

"Angel mist?" He questioned her words and Morgan hadn't realized she'd used them until after he repeated them.

"A long story." She laughed at her mistake and shrugged it off. "I had time to relax."

"That's something I would have paid to see."

Over a greasy plate of french fries and a sloppy hamburger Morgan demolished because she was famished, they talked for a long time. Evan watched as her eyes lit up like he'd never seen, there was a sparkle in them he hadn't noticed before, he realized it was because it had never been there before.

The more she talked, the more hopeful he became that the two of them could finally get past this and possibly take their relationship to the next level. He hadn't thought of his ex wife in months, all he'd thought about was Morgan, but he'd played along because if he had exposed his feelings he was afraid she would pull away from him. And take with her any chance he might have had.

So he'd remained a true friend, silent of his desires. Now she looked as if she'd be more open to something more between them. His heart began to pound louder in his chest and all he could think of was taking her in his arms and professing his love for her. That was until she said words that instantly shattered his hopes, gave him the reason for her happiness, whether she confessed it or not. As his heart began to soar with possibility, it crashed quickly.

"And Ryder was there." She said casually then shrugged her shoulders. "I thought it would be different. I'm not sure what I expected to happen."

"Did anything happen?"

Morgan remembered their night of passion, it was hard to keep from her mind. "I feel like we came to an understanding."

"Meaning?"

"Meaning we don't hate each other like we tried to do. It was easier for both of us to pretend we did, than it was to deal with what we had to deal with. And that was saying goodbye to each other."

He heard the words but he didn't see it in her face. They may have verbally said the word, but it would be a long time before she came to the same conclusion in her heart. She was still in love, he could see it. She may not have fully recovered from whatever she suffered, but Ryder was the cause of her transformation, of that he was sure. And although he teased it wouldn't matter if she were thinking of someone else the night they almost made love on the kitchen floor, he knew he couldn't actually live the rest of his life that way. And that's what he would have been pushing towards, a commitment from her, a future with her.

Evan was crushed. He could no longer pretend he didn't care for her, and she wouldn't be able to pretend she didn't still have strong feelings for another man. She would probably try, and that would hurt him more. He would step out of her way, step out of her life, and to save his heart from further breakage, he smiled broadly when he spoke.

"My ex wife and I are seeing each other again." His smile appeared genuine on the outside. "We've been out a few times and, well, we're starting to talk a little more. I think we might be on our way back together."

She was quiet for a moment, unsure what she thought about the news, but had to be happy for him. "Evan, that's great."

"It shouldn't change that much for us, I probably won't be able to call as often, and…"

"I'll be put on the Christmas card list your secretary sends out every year." Morgan sighed and took his hand. "It will change everything. You don't have to let me down easy, I wasn't even thinking that once that happened, I'd be left out in the cold."

"Never left out in the cold." He squeezed her hand, there was so much more he wanted to say but couldn't. "I don't know how it will work out, but I think I'd better not call for awhile. It would make it easier to not have something in the way…"

"You don't have to explain. I understand, Evan, I really do. I don't think your wife needs to have any suspicions about me, and it would be hard for her not to, even if there is no reason to."

"This is the easiest breakup I've ever had." He laughed even though he didn't want to.

"A simple, clean break. Who'd have ever thought such a thing existed?"

"I hope you find someone, Morgan. If it hadn't of been for my wife, I'd like to think it could have been me."

Morgan looked at Evan and realized how close they had become. She'd taken it for granted before, now she was losing him too. In that instant, she realized how much she would miss him. Why did living involve so many instances of letting go of things she didn't want to let go of?

"Maybe it could have been you." She said softly. Who knows what could have happened between them? Could he have been the one to help her forget Ryder? Something she wouldn't have to think about as she watched him walk out of her life also.

****

Nancy also mentioned a difference in her appearance when Morgan surprised her and showed up on her doorstep for a weekend visit.

"Aren't you a sight to behold?" Nancy opened the door wide and hugged her. "I was actually going to come into the city tomorrow and surprise you."

"Have a spare bed for the weekend? I was going to call, but I took the chance when I had it and escaped."

"You never need to call." Nancy stood back and admired a change in her. "You look fantastic. Did you do something to your hair? A spa treatment? What is it? I need to know."

"The fresh air of Alaska." She thought of the words Angel mist again but didn't say them.

"I'm calling the travel agent today."

Nancy could see the difference in her friend, her eyes were brighter and her smile was brighter, there was something missing from Morgan and with it gone, she saw her in a new light, even heard it as her laughter with the kids rang through the house like a song. That evening, after the girls were in bed, the two sat together over a glass of wine.

"I don't know what it is about you now, but I promise I won't bug you anymore about your life. You seem happier now, and that makes me happier. Before, you were just... I don't even know how to describe it, but I never thought you were happy."

"I wasn't," Morgan admitted. "But it didn't have anything to do with dating and not having a male companion like you suspected it was. That would never have been my cure no matter who you set me up with."

"And all it took was Alaska? I'd like to think Evan still figures in there somewhere."

Morgan looked at her oddly, thought she would have known. "Evan is getting back with his ex wife."

Nancy looked shocked. "That's impossible."

"I just saw him a few days ago."

"Morgan, his ex wife moved out of state months ago. I know for sure she hasn't been back, and even if she had, there's not a chance in hell he'd reunite with her."

Now Morgan looked shocked and confused. Why would he tell her that? Why would he make something like that up? She went on to explain the plan she'd devised the first night they set the two up, and ended with him telling her the news.

"We were never really seeing each other, not as dating anyway. It was all a ploy to get the two of you off our backs. It worked, and we became great friends from it, so why would he lie to me?"

Nancy was overwhelmed at the thought it had all been a ploy. "Well you two were certainly good actors, I never would have guessed it was all fake. And..." Nancy looked more confused now too. "And I don't know why he would have told you that about his wife."

"It wasn't like he had to break up with me, we weren't dating, it doesn't make any sense."

"You can say it was all a con for Ray and I, but he had feelings for you Morgan, I know he had real feelings for you. The way he talked about you, the way he looked when I asked him about you, I know these things."

Morgan thought back to the talk they had when he told her about his ex wife. They were talking of Alaska, about her trip, and then it dawned on her, they were talking about Ryder. Right after that he said he'd reunited with his wife.

"Ryder." Morgan said his name out loud, she understood then. "He pulled himself out, I guess he still suspected there was something between Ryder and I, and he pulled himself out before it was too late, he didn't want to be hurt." Then she thought of something else. "Maybe he just wanted me to figure it out on my own once and for all."

"Ryder? Isn't that the friend of yours from the conference? How did he get in the picture? What does he have to do with this?" Nancy poured another glass of wine for the both of them and sat up in her seat. "Okay, there's a lot more to this you're going to tell me."

Morgan could talk of it now, it didn't hurt as bad. She began to explain some things about her Nancy had never known, she finally revealed a mysterious past her friend had always wondered about. Each word of explanation gave Nancy insight and she came to better understand what haunted her, what stopped her from living before. It felt good for Morgan to release it as she told her everything from the accident to the cruise. She talked of May and their childhood, the relationship they shared as twins, and there were still tears that came to her eyes when she talked of her death.

"I used to wonder if she hadn't died in my arms if it would have been easier, but it still would have been just as hard." Morgan stepped over to the window and looked outside.

"I never knew you were in so much pain."

"I hid it well from everyone, even myself for a long time."

"And you and Ryder never got married."

"I ran away like a coward, I didn't have the strength to face my demons, especially not there in Beach Lake. I know the town didn't blame me now, that was only my own paranoia, I blamed myself and figured everyone else did too. Even Ryder and my mother, I figured out its why I could never mourn with them, the thought of taking away people they loved made me feel even guiltier."

"And you and Ryder now?" Morgan had explained the cruise, but she hadn't fully explained to Nancy exactly what happened between the two, where they stood now.

Morgan looked out of the window and thought she saw a flash of light from across the way. Probably a reflection from a street lamp, she couldn't be sure. "I thought I was supposed to dance again, but I was too late for Ryder, he has a life I'm not a part of now," she shrugged her shoulders. "Who knew it wasn't meant to be after all."

"Dance?" Nancy questioned.

"It was something May said to me before she died, and I'm not even sure what it means other than I would get past their deaths."

"It has to mean more than that, and just because Ryder has a life now, that doesn't mean you won't dance again, who's to say it was meant to be with Ryder? Maybe Evan's the one you're supposed to dance with."

Could it be? Through their own pain, both of the men had tried to help her in the best way they knew how, both of them let her go, but it had been at great sacrifice to themselves. In the aftermath of that, Ryder found himself with another. Maybe it wasn't his initial intention to fully release her, she truly believed he held out hope for as long as he could, but she couldn't fault him, couldn't fault a man for choosing to live when Morgan hadn't. He used to keep his window open only for her to come inside, that window was closed now.

She looked back and recalled things about Evan, could now see the true feelings he had, and had she not been so wrapped up in her past haunts she could have seen herself opening up to him, perhaps their relationship would have moved in a different direction. Evan cared for her, worried about her, was a compassionate man who'd waited patiently for her to get through her demons. He was the gallant sir she teased him to be at times, he'd stepped out of the way in order for Morgan to come to terms with her past and Ryder. He could see she hadn't, could probably see the feelings she still had for him.

It was hard to let go, when Morgan thought about it, she assumed that once the haze she'd been living in had lifted, her life would just go on where it left off. She had adjustments to make now, everything had changed, and she believed Evan did what he did in order for her to find her way first. He had to know she would find out it had been untrue, Nancy and Ray would have told her he hadn't gone back to his wife, so he knew she would eventually put the pieces together and go to him when she was finally ready.

Maybe it was now time for Morgan to let go of one thing and accept another, maybe it was time for her to dance again, to dance like the ballerina. May's words came back to her as she lay dying on the ground and Morgan held her for as long as she could.

'You'll dance, Morgan, you'll dance.' Morgan had picked her sister's battered head up gently, felt an open hole in the back of her skull and could feel the bone on her tender palm as warm blood covered it immediately, and there was so much blood. She felt it in her hand, sat in a puddle of it around her on the hard ground, and even though May's face appeared not to have been damaged at all, blood trickled in a steady stream from her mouth.

"You will too, May, you can't go anywhere, hang on."

"Like the ballerina..." May sputtered more. "The ballerina in the music box."

Nancy watched her friend's attention wander elsewhere, her eyes peeled to somewhere outside of the window. "Morgan?"

As she looked to the dark night outside, she saw the reflection of light she thought she'd seen before, but it wasn't her imagination, it was a definite reflection and a small beam came into the room. Nancy either couldn't see it, or hadn't noticed, and when Morgan turned it seemed to shine off the box, Amy's small wooden box. She walked to it and picked the box up slowly.

"What is that thing doing down here again? Last I saw it, it was in Amy's room and I told her to throw it away, it's still broken." Nancy said from beside her.

Morgan was afraid to open it but knew she had to. When she did, the ballerina danced just as she suspected it would, she twirled and spun in all her glory, and if one was to investigate and look, they would find that the wind mechanism on the bottom was fully wound down. There would have been no logical reason for it to work, no explanation to why she danced as the soft melody of the music filled the room, but there had been no logic to anything that was happening to her lately.

"It's fixed now," Morgan said softly, her whisper barely audible.

"That's the strangest thing." Nancy looked on in wonder, her voice a whisper also.

"Strange things happen."

As she held it, there was a reflection of light upon it, it was quick and again, Nancy didn't seem to notice. When she looked outside the window she didn't see anything, so where had the reflection come from?

Sometimes you didn't see things until it was too late, was she going to make the same mistake's she'd made in her past? Was she going to be blind and numb and allow life to go on around her? She'd let so many things slip through her hands, so many things lost to her, and Morgan knew that if she was truly going to live again, she had to completely settle things in her heart. Morgan continued to hold the box in her hand and knew what May wanted her to do and she could no longer deny her, Morgan knew it was time to dance again.

"I have to go," she said.

"Go where? You were supposed to stay the weekend. You can't go back to the city now."

Morgan's voice was the lightest of whispers. "I'm not going back to the city."

CHAPTER SEVENTEEN

Something pushed her forward to settle things. It was almost a physical force she could feel and she wondered what the urgency was. Would she be too late again? Her timing off and she would forever be one step behind?

"What are you doing in the country?" Evan asked as he opened the door.

"I surprised Nancy." She had a knowing look on her face and he looked a little guilty for his lie. "I'm glad I did, we had an enlightening chat."

"Come on in." He opened the door wider and she stepped inside. "I figured you'd find out sooner or later, I just didn't know it would be so soon."

"I'm sorry it's so late."

"Never too late for you, I was up."

He made a pot of coffee and they sat in his comfortable kitchen as everything came out. His love for her that had grown, how they couldn't truly move forward until she finally put Ryder and her past behind her, and just as she suspected, Evan had stepped out of the way in order for her to come to the conclusions she needed to.

"That's very chivalrous of you, my gallant sir." She smiled and teased. She thought of Amy's words then, said it was supposed to be like Cinderella, a fairy tale, and one would be whisked away by a dashing prince. "Most men would have fought with a vengeance."

"I can battle most things, but it would have been battling you, and I couldn't do that. You had to settle your battles first."

"I've been fighting with myself for years now, and it's been a tough war." She touched his face then, "And you've been so understanding, knowing things about me I was afraid to admit to myself. Forcing me to realize I can either hold on to a man I once loved and continue living in the past, or accept things the way they are now and go on from here."

"You look a little more settled now, even from the last time I saw you."

"It's still a little confusing at times, but I am more settled, I know what I have to do."

Evan looked at her for a long time, her hand soft upon his cheek and maybe he should have waited, but she had to know what his intentions were, had to know what he offered her. "Will you marry me?"

From behind him in the window, Morgan saw a flash of light from something, but outside of the window she knew there was nothing but trees. It seemed to flash frantically and she knew it was her sign from

May and Morgan wanted to openly sigh. Verbally wanted to answer her sister, 'I know, May, don't be so impatient.'

****

Morgan pulled up to the house and sat in the car for a few moments. The house looked quiet and still, no activity at all but she got out and approached the door. When she knocked, she heard nothing, and it didn't sound like anyone was inside or on the way to answer it.

She waited, but no noises could be heard, knocked again but it was the same quiet and when she looked through the thin curtain of the window she could see nothing. Then she walked off the porch to the front yard and looked to curtain closed windows throughout the rest of the home, it was obvious there was no one there.

There was no car in the drive and as she looked down the street, few people were out and about. A passing neighbor walking two dogs, rather two dogs walking him and she looked down the other direction to see a woman jogging. Other than that, it seemed only her until the paper boy whizzed by on rollerblades and Morgan had to wonder about the day long past when they delivered the paper on bicycles. She stepped closer to the sidewalk and looked up to the house again as if she'd see something different but she didn't. There was definitely no one there.

"Hey lady, watcha' doing?" The boy on the roller blades whizzed up to her then and questioned her motives.

She smiled at his protectiveness of his street. "I was looking for the people who lived here."

He eyed her suspiciously before he answered. "Who are you?"

"An old friend."

He hesitated, looked at her for a few moments, and then was satisfied he could trust her. "They're out of town, think they'll be back later today though."

She looked disappointed, Morgan wanted to see her home, wanted to finally face it, and remembered Ryder telling her his parents had liked the new owner. She didn't want to just knock on the door unexpected. Then she decided he could possibly help her after all. This was Beach Lake, everyone knew everyone. "Do you know their son Ryder? I think he lives in the city now but I don't know where."

"That's easy, Mr. Ryder lives back there in the old Bailey house." He pointed in the direction behind Ryder's boyhood home.

The old Bailey house, she'd used the term for other houses when she was young, the houses always had names and she imagined her old home would for generations be known as the 'old Bailey house', no matter who lived in it.

She looked to the young guy as if he'd just said the oddest thing. "Are you sure?"

"I just delivered his paper. He's already working."

"Working?"

"He has a company come in, but on the weekends he does some work himself. He's doing some remodeling and I help him out some," he beamed proud. "He pays me five bucks an hour and even lets me use the saw sometimes."

Morgan's concentration centered on the boy's words, Ryder living in the 'old Bailey house', her home, how could that be? How could she not have known? Again, there were many things she didn't make herself aware of in the daze she'd buried herself in for so long. It wasn't what she expected, wasn't where she expected to find Ryder, and it took her a few moments to let it sink in. He'd bought her mother's house, her childhood home. Had he bought it for Stella? Few homes ever sold in Beach Lake, they were held onto by generations, so he wouldn't have had much of a choice to pick from. Were they married now? He was probably remodeling because Stella's taste would be more modern. Knock off the creaky old back porch and make an enormous sunroom, put in a huge master suite with a fancy bathroom and marble tub, she could hear her voice in her head, the distaste she would have for the old fashioned things in life.

She didn't seem the type to appreciate the character of the house. Wouldn't see the old stone fireplace with its massive mantle as an asset, she'd probably have it demolished and replaced with a white wall and a flat gas fireplace operated by remote. The wide planked floor in the kitchen would be ripped out and covered with an imported stone tile. No, Morgan couldn't see her appreciating the 'old Bailey house' just the way it was.

As with all old houses, the house certainly could use some improvements, but it began to anger her a little that Ryder would let something like that happen to her house. Maybe he was erasing every trace of the past, maybe he was doing things he needed to do, just like herself, to get past this line in her life. And it wasn't her house anymore, she'd let that slip through her hands as she'd done so many things, and he could do what he wanted.

"You know where the old Bailey house is, don't ya?" The boy asked and brought her back from her thoughts.

"Everyone knows where the old Bailey house is, don't they?"

"Did you know Ms. Bea too?" He looked at her with more curiosity.

She smiled then. "You could say that."

"You from around here?"

"Used to be."

"Ms. Bea used to give out the best Halloween candy. She was cool, I used to cut her lawn after school and she always had the best ice cream."

"Vanilla and she puts it inside half a cantaloupe."

He beamed. "You do know Ms. Bea."

Morgan looked down the block and saw old Mr. Green standing in the front yard waiting for his paper. He timed it perfectly, always had, and knew it was there at a specific time, if it wasn't he stood and waited. She knew because she used to be the paper girl and would catch heck all the time.

"You'd better go, Mr. Green will stand out there in his robe all day and wait."

"When I used to ride my bike, my chain broke one day and he was standing there till noon." The boy looked back to her. "Hey, how'd you know he does that?"

"Like I said, I used to be from around here."

"I'd better go so Mr. Green can go back inside." He began to move off and turned back around, spoke over his shoulder. "See ya, lady."

"See ya, kid."

She smiled as she looked after him when he whizzed past Mr. Green who stood in his old blue robe and white knee socks. The paper was thrown almost directly in front of him and he bent down, picked it up, and went back inside and shut the door. It was nice to know some things never changed. While she'd been fighting her demons, they had all lived their day to day lives with no deviation, there was something to be said for consistency. They'd built something solid here, something as strong and unbreakable as the largest old oak in town that sat in her backyard, rather Ryder's backyard.

She left her car at his parent's house, and instead of driving around, Morgan would take the way she was familiar with, through the back yard, through the small patch of trees, and over the fence. As she made her way to the fence, what waited on the other side almost made her consider turning back. But it wasn't waiting for her, it was there, and she'd been waiting to return to it. It was her final step in recovery, her final healing to get past that line in her life.

How difficult would it be for her to face Ryder and Stella, in their new life, in their new home, her home? She was stronger now, but was she strong enough to actually see it? Maybe it would be better if she didn't.

It was a familiar route, but it wouldn't be easy. She walked through the yard and to the back, but when she got to the small patch of trees she realized how long it had actually been. The path between the two houses was not as defined as it used to be. She knew the way by heart and barreled straight ahead, but it was now overgrown with branches that snagged her hair and thorns reached out and scratched her arm, as if they were alive and grabbed her viciously. She'd caught her pants leg on a downed tree when she had to climb over it and ripped a gaping hole.

It was so much easier when she was younger, now it felt as if she were crawling through a combat war zone. By the time she reached the high fence she saw the boards that had been nailed in years ago were halfway rotted and wondered if she would break her neck if she attempted it. Morgan took a moment to ponder going around the long way, parallel to the fence until the clearing, but after surveying it she knew it was useless. There was nothing but dense brush and trees, the old path was no longer there and she didn't have the patience to go back and walk around on the street.

The first few boards she placed her foot on weren't bad, they supported her, but almost to the top one gave way and broke as she clung to the top to keep herself from falling hard to the ground. Left with no choice, she swung her leg over the fence, there was no turning back and she wasn't sure what was on the other side as her leg dangled.

She shouldn't have been in such a hurry, should have at least taken it slow. Her foot felt for something and nothing was there, she had to swing her other leg over and take her chances. When she did she knew there was absolutely nothing to brace her foot on, then she felt herself falling to the ground but was stopped with strong arms that broke the fall, possibly saving her from a broken leg or two.

Ryder laughed at both the sight of Morgan's dirty and battered clothes and the surprised look on her face, his face held just as much surprise. "Talk about a drop in guest. You're the last person I expected to see hopping over my fence this morning." He laughed as he pulled a leaf out of her hair. "You look like shit."

"A red eye flight from Minneapolis, I've been up all night."

"It doesn't have anything to do with the flight."

Morgan looked down at herself. "Am I that old that I can't make it through the woods anymore? My workouts are easier than that."

He looked at the disheveled Morgan before him, dirt smudged her face and clothes and her top was torn. "We could do a lot of things when we were younger, you aren't ten anymore."

"Age does have a way of creeping up on us, doesn't it? I don't mean to drop in on you like this." Morgan laughed at the literal words.

"And over the fence, just the sight of you hanging there made my day."

"It used to be much easier. Was that fence always that high?" She looked back to it again as if it had been replaced with a taller one but knew it hadn't. Then she brushed her clothes off as best she could. In doing so, she hit a scrape on her hand and realized she was bleeding a little.

Ryder took her hand and looked at her wound. "Let's go inside and clean that up, I have something I can put on it."

"I don't..." Morgan wasn't sure she'd want to walk inside and see Stella in her home, in her life. "I don't want to interrupt. I would have called first, but I didn't know where you lived, so when I got to town I went to your mom and dad's."

"Are they back this early? I didn't expect them till later today."

"No, the paperboy told me you lived here."

He looked at her and realized it was the first realization she'd had of it, from a paperboy on the street. "I thought Bea would have told you by now."

"She's quite distracted with Jerry in her life, if she weren't riding bulls in Texas, the subject probably would have come up."

He chuckled at the thought. "Riding bulls?"

"A mechanical one, but she rode it."

He pulled another piece of debris out of her hair, this time a small stick. "When she mentioned selling the house, I knew I had to have it. You can never buy anything in Beach Lake, most times it's willed to you." He pointed over to the work he'd been doing, the boards he was cutting that sat on sawhorses in the back yard. "I'm remodeling the basement into offices, going to open my own practice here."

Morgan wondered if Stella were a doctor too, how odd he was able to keep the dream they once had for themselves. Perhaps fate had a way of righting itself when it had gone wrong.

Ryder felt he needed to explain himself when she said nothing. "Bea was insistent you wanted no parts of the house, I was sure of that before I went through with it. As a matter of fact, when I was positive she was going to sell it, I just told her I knew someone who wanted to buy it and set it all up through a lawyer. I thought if she knew it was me, she'd lower the price, make it cheaper. Which she tried to do when she found out but I wouldn't let her."

"Someone else may have seen it as opportunity to take advantage of a single widowed woman. I'm glad she had someone she could trust and someone to help her through it." She still felt a small tinge of guilt she hadn't been there for her mother. "Are you doing all the work yourself?"

"I've hired someone, but they don't work fast enough so I do what I can on the weekends." He looked to her and wondered how long he would have to wait for her to reveal the reason she was there.

Morgan felt blood as it trickled down her arm from a large thorn bush scrape and raised it to look. "Do you have a rag I could borrow?"

He pulled one that hung from his pants pocket. "A dirty one, but I think I can do better than that. Come inside and let me put something on it. I am a doctor, so if you don't mind that I don't have my white jacket on, I might be able to fix it up for you."

She hesitated as she looked towards the house.

"You still can't go inside?"

"It actually isn't that, I... I don't want to interrupt anything. I was just trying to be considerate. I know how unexpected company can be."

"Unexpected company? You'll never be company in this house." He watched as she still hesitated. "If you didn't come to see the house, did you come to get something out of it?"

"Something like that." Morgan's gaze was taken to the house, she wanted to look to her sister's window to see if her face would be there again, but as she looked up she discovered the window was fully open. "What's that window doing open?"

Ryder looked in the direction of it also. "Oddest thing, before I left on the cruise I painted that room and I couldn't get that window open at all. Came home and it was wide open, no break in or anything, just wide open and now I can't get it down. Is there a trick to it or something?"

"No trick." Morgan answered with a knowing whisper.

"Then you can do me the favor and close it while you're here. Come on, let's go get both those scratches of yours and the window taken care of if you think it's so easy. I want to see this, I've been trying for weeks." Ryder walked ahead of her and Morgan followed.

As she crossed the yard, she looked around but didn't feel the panic of before, she let the memories in this time, let them soothe her. The screen door creaked and slammed shut and she heard her father say he would have to fix that one day. She was glad it hadn't been fixed.

The instant she stepped into the kitchen, it was stepping directly into her past and she was flooded with the memories of a more happy time but she embraced them and didn't push it away. Everything was much the way Bea left it. Ryder didn't have enough to fill the big house and Bea had still been hesitant to completely clean it out before she left. Eventually things would be packed away and stored in the attic for her, given away, whatever she wanted to do with it. But in the meantime, the home was as if time had covered it with a dome and preserved it.

They walked up the stairs and Morgan opened the door to May's old room. It looked just as she remembered even with the fresh coat of paint, but there was quite a bit less of May's personal things. There were no stuffed toys from her younger years or drawings of fashion on the wall as she got older. It was the same furniture and the bare minimum of anything else. Material things weren't needed to know she'd been there.

On the small stand by the window, she saw the wooden box, the ballerina box. She also noticed a slight rainbow reflection of light but

Morgan couldn't decipher where it came from, there was nothing to cause a reflection, and as she stared, it faded away.

She walked over to the window that was wide open and Morgan felt that when she let her spirit go in Alaska, May freed her own spirit from the house. Not only had she left it open to signify her departure, she'd left the window open for her to come inside, just as Ryder used to do. Was it all coincidence? She couldn't deny it was strange, but it was more than that. As Jerry would say, it was like a big ole' grizzly coming for her, only now her eyes were open wide enough to see what it meant. May drove her home, she needed to be there for a final healing, Morgan was sure of it.

Maybe it was something she'd made up in her mind, just as the Northern Lights and the dance of the spirits she wished to believe, but whether it were true or not, didn't matter. She knew May was no longer there, but knew she heard her wherever she was as Morgan whispered silently in her mind... 'I'm home now, May, you can go home too.'

The slightest of breezes wafted through the window, though it was a still day outside and the leaves on the trees hadn't moved. After she said a silent final farewell she reached up and easily pulled the window down, it was smooth and closed with no effort.

Ryder just watched from the doorway.

"Nothing to it," Morgan turned and said with a smile.

"There's a trick you're not going to tell me, that window was stuck. I almost broke the pane trying to force it."

Morgan smiled and turned her attention back to the outside once more. May would have hounded her forever had she not returned and faced this part of her life, put closure on the pain she felt from the house and remember all that was good there.

She then picked up the box she knew so well, a box similar to one many little girls had. As she opened it, of course the ballerina twirled in her glory, just as she suspected it would. Morgan stood for a long time as the music filled the room.

"You tripped an awful lot." Ryder said softly as he leaned against the doorjamb, knew what she was thinking about.

Morgan looked up to him. "How do you know? We never danced when you were around."

"I used to laugh my head off watching you. I could see you through the big window sometimes when you were downstairs. May was as graceful as a swan."

She chuckled lightly, her voice tender. "I'll be the first to admit I was quite the opposite, I hated it. I only did it for her."

"She knew you hated it, but she knew you loved her and would do it anyway."

It struck Morgan she'd never figured that out. Even then, May knew it would be difficult for Morgan to come back to the house, but knew she'd do it anyway. "You knew us both so well."

"I thought it was fascinating, identical twins that were total opposites in personality." Ryder watched her face, it didn't upset her, and she could talk about it now.

They went to the kitchen where Ryder began the task of skillfully cleaning and bandaging her wounds. There was a few small surface scrapes, but also a large one that was a little deeper that needed to be cleaned well to prevent infection. Like one of the many children he'd healed, Morgan stood like a foolish child. She'd been mended many times in this kitchen from childhood injuries, but always by her mother, never by Ryder.

"I probably should have driven around, but I just did it automatically, didn't even think about it."

"We do that sometimes." He didn't want to tell her all the things he'd automatically done over time thinking she was right there beside him. "Isn't the first time you've scraped yourself up. You always used to barrel through like one of Jerry's bulls. I used to think you were still afraid of the giant super sized groundhog you convinced yourself you saw one night."

"I did see it, it was huge."

"And it had fangs." He said the words blandly and shook his head at the ridiculous thought. "Fangs."

"And he's probably still there waiting for me, I wouldn't have attempted it at night, not without a machete anyway, it's overgrown a bit." She relished the feel of his soothing touch. "Wonder why our parents never put in a path and a gate."

"We wouldn't let them. It was an adventure in the woods. We called it the woods anyway, nothing but a thick patch of trees."

"With a mysterious fanged groundhog that lives in it," she added.

He laughed at the thought again. "I think that was the only thing that ever scared you in your life, and it wasn't even real."

At that moment she was a little scared of Stella walking in and wondering what she was doing in her kitchen. It would put a damper on her homecoming, put a damper on her memory of this house, she wanted to see it and experience just as it was, not with someone new such as Stella.

Morgan looked to his supplies. "You're medicine cabinet is so much more well equipped than mine. I think I have a few Band-Aids if I have that." Morgan raised her arm as he wiped gently with a solution.

"I'm a pediatrician, cuts, burns and scrapes is a constant and keeping a good supply on hand isn't an option. I went through a case a week of this stuff when Billy Myers first started to use those roller blades."

She smiled. "The paperboy? Cute kid. Myers," she thought about the name. "Could that be Ricky Myers little boy?"

"The same."

"He's gotten so big, I didn't even recognize him."

They chatted for a few moments about a few others. Ryder answered her questions and in the back of his mind, constantly wondered what she was doing there.

"So how have you been?" She asked with interest and waited for him to say something about her, something about Stella.

"I'm fine. You?"

"That's a normal standard answer. A standard answer for strangers or people you're passing on the street. I come all this way and make it past the fanged groundhog, I can't get a real answer?" She said it with a playful defiant tone and repeated it when he didn't answer. "So? Do I get a real answer? How are you?"

"We're doctors, we're busy." He didn't look at her as he discarded one cotton pad for a new one and went back to work. "I know, 'busy' is another standard answer too."

What she didn't know was that Ryder referred to the two of them with his answer, not Stella, but the words hit her that way. The thought of Stella being a doctor, the two of them with their own practice in Beach Lake, now in her old home, how could one so easily be substituted?

CHAPTER EIGHTEEN

Ryder finished his work and stepped away from her. "That should be enough so that we won't have to amputate."

"Am I your first in-house patient? Do I at least get a plague or something on the wall? A reminder that I was here?"

"I'll charge you one dollar for being my first official patient and then I'll frame it." He looked to her and laughed. "Or maybe you'd rather have a lollipop."

"You give out lollipops?" She chuckled at the thought of this muscular handsome man with a lollipop in his hand.

"Have to bribe them sometimes, besides, I have a few dentist friends that can use the business."

Ryder put his supplies away and they stood in an uncomfortable silence, he had taken a reserved stance, wasn't going to make assumptions for why she was there and told himself to merely wait for the explanation of what she wanted.

"Thanks." She tried to smile and succeeded in a feeble way. "I should go. I really didn't want to intrude."

"Did you just come to Beach Lake to climb the fence one more time?"

"I'm not sure why I came, maybe I shouldn't have. I just had a feeling I needed to be here, to see it once more." She shrugged her shoulders. "I think I saw it as a final step in recovery, to be able to face it now when I couldn't before."

"You're looking well." Ryder had noticed the difference in her, she'd let go of so many things, didn't look distant and haunted by what had happened.

"I'm much better than I used to be."

"I can see." He smiled, she did look good, the fear of life was no longer in her eyes. "Well, you're here now, might as well stay and look around. I've got work to do, stay as long as you want, I'll either be outside or in the basement."

"Thanks," she said. "But you don't have to leave."

"You came to see the house, feel free and take your time. If you want something else, take whatever it is, everything's much the way your mother left it."

Morgan hesitated for a moment and then spoke. "I don't know if it's here or not, I don't even know whatever happened to it, but have you come across the wedding dress?"

There it was, her reason for being there revealed. She was to marry Evan and she'd do it in the dress her sister designed and created for her, a wedding dress no one had ever been allowed to see except for May. Ryder couldn't stop the stone reserve that overtook him.

"I've never seen it. Your mother may have put it in the attic somewhere and you can check the closets." He had to leave the room then, had to get away from her. "I've got work to do."

She stood in the kitchen for a long time before she ventured elsewhere, was surprised at the calm feeling being there gave her, she felt comfort, a calm tranquil feeling she allowed to come inside and fill her. Morgan let it envelope her and make her feel safe, just as it always had.

Morgan felt truly peaceful for the first time in a long time. On that quiet Sunday morning in the stillness, as the world carried on around them, Morgan let that feeling in, the link to her final healing. She walked around and let the memories in, memories she hadn't been able to let in before.

There were a few small changes, a new set of chairs in the living room, new curtains here and there, things she questioned whether they'd been Stella's changes or perhaps her mother had purchased them. She wouldn't know, she hadn't walked into that house in over four years so she was unsure.

As she stood in the hallway of the second floor she heard the voices of long ago, their mother calling them downstairs for dinner, their father as he came home and shut the door. She and May would race to be first to greet him. She heard the giggles in the night, in her mind pictured them both sitting on the bed and the chatter of young teens. It was as if the house was actually a living, breathing thing, and the memories and what was inside its fuel for sustenance to keep it alive. As if it too thrived on the life inside its walls, both past and present.

Standing on the landing about to go downstairs again, something made her turn around and look upwards to the third floor. The door at the top had light underneath, but how could that be? It was a room with no window. As she walked up the creaky steps the light seemed to fade and it was dark again. It was quiet and still and she opened the door wider to let the light from the stairs in and then turned on the small lamp. May had used it as her sewing room, her design room, and when she opened the closet door there were several things covered in clothes bags, and though concealed, the wedding dress was unmistakable.

Morgan retrieved it and lay it down on the empty table and unzipped the most exquisite thing she'd ever seen. The top was very fitted with off the shoulder sleeves, and she'd used the lace from their mother's wedding dress, an imported cream lace with the most intricate hand beading. She traced the pattern with her finger, felt the hand sewn stitching so meticulous and perfect, crafted with such love and care.

The skirt portion was like a cloud of ivory, full and glorious, as she continued to pull it from the bag and it spewed out into the room all around her. It reminded her of a much larger version of the ballet dress May would always make her wear and she laughed.

Morgan had never seen anything so grand and lavish, it was truly a creation to behold in all its splendor as she held it close to her body, looked in the mirror with awe. Although she'd always hated the ballerina tutu's, the dress was the most fitting thing she would never have imagined for herself, it wouldn't have been something she would have picked out, would have been the farthest thing she pictured. And yet as she looked at the reflection there wouldn't have been anything else more perfect, nothing else would have suited her.

For one instant, she thought she saw May's reflection in the mirror behind her, a satisfied look of contentment in her smile. It was very faint and of course when Morgan turned around the vision was no longer there. Morgan let her hand sway down the huge skirt of the dress then she pulled it close and hugged it to her as she closed her eyes. May would never really be gone, a part of her spirit would always be there with Morgan, she knew she'd never have to completely let go.

May and her father had shown her the way home. The place she needed to be to complete the process of healing, to come to terms and accept the changes in all their lives. A few short months ago, she didn't feel like she had the fight in her, but she was strong again now, strong enough to fight for what was hers and Morgan was home again, and home to stay. She'd come too far to give up now.

Overcoming obstacles served to shape our lives, if everything were easy it wouldn't be so entertaining and funny. Some of Jerry's words came to her, he also used the term 'flies on shit' and other eloquent endearments, but her subconscious had absorbed things. Morgan took a deep breath and knew what she had to do, she had to lay it all on the line, and Ryder had to know she wanted to claim what was hers.

She found him in the basement and stood silent for a long time, watched him as he worked vigilantly. Sweat poured from his body and he was dirty as sawdust clung to it. There was no question now signs and spirits had pushed her there, it all made sense. Morgan watched for a long time through the dusty distance. He cut lumbar and was building a wall and it was a long time before he turned to see her standing there. When he turned the saw off the room became still and quiet.

After he left her in the kitchen, Ryder had gone back to work with a vengeance. He wasn't sure how much time passed as he sawed, nailed and sanded. Wasn't even sure if he was doing it correctly, the thought of her being there sent his mind and emotions in a chaotic frenzy, the thought of what she'd come for sent him into a rage that burned his soul.

Let her take the dress and leave for her new life. As a matter of fact, he thought to himself, he should call a trucking company right then and have them come and she could take everything, every little piece of herself that was there. He didn't know how he'd get rid of the piece of her that was imbedded inside, but he would learn somehow. She had, so it wasn't as impossible as it seemed.

What had he been thinking? After the cruise and her beginning to heal, regardless what he'd told Bea, he did have hope, thought that once she fully healed she would be able to come back to him, to finally come home. He'd waited patiently, just as he'd done when she left him the first time. But she'd gone back to Minneapolis with other things in mind and she was now ready to go on with her life, her life with someone else.

His anger escalated into a boil, but as he looked to her now, he saw something strange in her eyes, knew how difficult it must have been for her. He still worried about her and supposed he always would.

"You okay?" He said with concern, even though a little gruffly because the more time he had alone, the angrier he had become. Now he just wanted her to leave, thought she would have snuck out the door with what she'd come for, her wedding dress, and that would be the end of it. Just as she left long ago, only then, she didn't take anything with her, not even the memory of him.

"Yeah, I'm okay."

He wiped his forehead and walked over to her. "Did you get what you wanted?"

"I can't take anything from here, everything that's here belongs here."

He nodded and waited for more words to come, didn't want to speak himself, knew he was on the verge of explosion, but she didn't leave and he didn't want her to linger. "If you change your mind, it isn't going anywhere for awhile, if there's anything you want it can be shipped." He still wanted to call a mover and insist she take it then.

"I won't change my mind," she said it with conviction.

Ryder wanted her to leave but she stood there longer, lowered her head and seemed to shift nervously. He knew there was more and he prepared himself for the blow as she finally spoke again.

"I don't know if it's possible, but I belong here too, and I'm not sure what can be done about that."

He looked at her with coldness, the thought of Morgan ever moving back to Beach Lake wasn't something he'd considered. Not moving back with another man, it was him she was to come home to, him she was to love, but now she would begin her new life and wanted the house back. She'd come to claim it again and he wanted to vent his rage, wanted to scream and yell but the absurdity of it, the absurdity of the way they'd turned out made him quiet instead. He didn't know what to say, so he said nothing.

Every instinct told him to fight her on it. The home was his now, she'd let her mother sell it to what she thought was a stranger. But she'd come looking for her wedding dress and seen the opportunity to get it back when she found out it was him that owned it now. She had deserted their dream, why couldn't she let him fulfill his part of it? But she wanted it back now to fulfill her own dreams, new dreams he wasn't part of, just when Ryder thought he'd suffered more pain then he'd ever known, another excruciating jab tore through his heart. Even though in his mind he defended him being there, how could he fight her? Ryder knew in his heart, what was left of it, he wouldn't fight her.

Morgan stood and watched his cold stance, the distance of him grow further and further away from her. She'd said it, lay her feelings out, offered herself to him with no assurances he'd want her in return and she stood with bared soul and naked emotion. She waited for him to say something but suspected it wasn't the words of love she wanted to hear. He didn't love her anymore. How could she have been so foolish to think he would welcome her into his life again after everything she'd done to him? The excited feeling in the pit of her stomach turned to a gut wrenching ache.

"I know it isn't something you expected, but…" she stammered, stopped talking and waited for something else to happen. Where was May? Where was her father? How could she have been so wrong?

"No, I wasn't expecting it. But then again, I don't expect anything you throw at me. You'd think I should be used to it by now but it still takes me by surprise." He finally managed to speak and his words lashed out with bitterness.

"I know I've hurt you before, but…"

"But you haven't had enough and just need to pop in and out of my life on a whim to screw it up." He turned then, would let her have what she'd come for and maybe he would move to Minneapolis now, somewhere, anywhere, far away from Beach Lake.

"I know this might put a kink in your plans for…" She was going to say for him and Stella, but every time she tried to speak he interrupted, how could Morgan fight for what was hers if he wouldn't let her?

"A kink in my plans? Not at all, you didn't think I'd been doing all this work for me, did you?" He shouted sarcastically with a cynical laugh. "Of course not, I've been doing it all for you and Evan. It's the least I could do for you."

"Me and…"

Ryder turned away and went back to hammering. "Can you give me some time to at least finish the disaster I've created in the basement? I'll need at least a few weeks to get the walls up for you. You can call an attorney and get the paperwork started, by the time everything's done I'll have it back to livable. It's your house, Morgan, take it."

It took her a few moments of total confusion to realize he didn't have a clue what she was talking about and he thought she wanted the house back. As her heart began to fall and crack at the thought of his rejection of her, it did another of its roller coaster turns and began to lift again. She walked over and stopped his hammering by placing her hand on his bare arm, the feel of him connected them like nothing else.

"Ryder, you don't understand."

He turned with anger in his eyes. "No, I don't understand, but if you want the house back, it's yours and I won't fight you on it. You belong here more than I do."

"I don't belong here without you." She got the words out quickly before he could interrupt or turn away from her again.

Ryder had suppressed his hope she would be there for that reason, convinced himself otherwise, and now faced with it, it took several minutes for it to sink in.

Morgan laughed at the mistake they'd both been thinking. "I guess you were right about the way Jerry is, if we said things we meant, things would be simple." She pressed to him, wouldn't let him interrupt again. "I love you Ryder, I..."

But he did manage to interrupt, Ryder didn't let her speak, he heard the words of love he'd longed to hear once again and it was all he needed. When his lips touched hers every miserable day of the last years totally dissolved into oblivion as if they'd never existed, as if the tormented days of his suffering had all been a bad dream.

When he pulled away from her she could see her entire life in his eyes once more. It was where she'd left her dreams for safe keeping, where her heart lie, all right here in his arms. And he'd held onto it for safekeeping, held it for her even though he didn't know if she'd ever return for it. In the dirty lumber strewn basement full of sawdust and new beginnings they would start their life again.

She put her hand on his face and touched the familiar cheek, felt it down to her soul as if it were her own skin. "After all I've put you through, after all this time, it took an overgrown cowboy to teach me that if I'm not living, I'm dying. I want to live again, and I live with you. It doesn't matter where I am physically, I'm always with you."

Ryder didn't say anything, couldn't say anything. He pictured her taking her wedding dress and leaving then thought she wanted the house back. Had convinced himself of that, having her in his arms was the furthest thing from his mind, wasn't what he expected and he kissed her again for assurances. The feel of her, the words he'd waited so long for, they all came through.

The connection of their souls reunited. It was how it was meant to be, how it was supposed to be, she'd been told and pushed in this direction and she knew she'd never have any say about it, she would always be called home.

"I guess we're going to have to clear a path and put in a gate if you're going to be visiting your in-laws. We'd use all of our medical supplies patching you up all the time." Ryder held her tighter and their worlds became one again.

"I never really meant to leave you, I always…"

"Morgan," he stopped her. "You never left me. You needed to do what you had to do, you left Beach Lake but you never truly left my soul."

Morgan knew that, it wasn't only because of May and her father, they weren't the only one's to lead her there. "You led me home, Ryder." She could see the confusion on his face. "Remember we used to use the flashlights at night?"

His face looked a little guilty. "I've never admitted it, but I never understood any signals, you gave me an entire notebook of code you'd made up but I just flashed the light."

She touched his face with tenderness. "We didn't need to know what the flashes meant, it was a connection and that's all that mattered, I'm just sorry it took me so long to get here."

"Shhhh… you're here now." He placed his finger over her lips. "No more apologies. This was how it was meant to be, all of it. Maybe had we not been apart so long, we wouldn't have been strong enough to hold on. Who knows why it happened the way it did but we're here now, doesn't matter how we got here."

"Back to the beginning of the dreams we had for ourselves."

Ryder laughed at the surroundings of construction mayhem, broken boards and debris all around. "The beginning? We're standing in the middle of it."

They couldn't see it, but the reflection of light from an unknown source appeared through the dirty, grimy basement window and shone on them through the dusty haze. Then it was gone just as quickly as it appeared.

Printed in the United States
202281BV00002B/17/A

9 780976 148050